She was taking a shower, getting clean.

While he was hot, sweaty, dirty and felt pretty much like he'd been hired out to be on a chain gang, not raffled as someone's dream date. Definitely not appreciated.

And, unfortunately, not very well equipped to look good while he was mucking around doing chores the rest of the male world could probably complete with one hand tied behind their backs.

He had a huge pull in the front of his brand-new designer shirt, a cartoon bandage on his elbow, smears of dirt all over his khaki slacks and it seemed that he'd somehow gotten something *green* stuck in his hair that Janna hadn't bothered to tell him about.

He could cheerfully strangle the woman.

What really bothered him, and what he really wished he wouldn't be considering, or worrying about, was what a really rotten impression he must be making on Janna Monroe.

Not that he liked her…

Dear Reader,

There's something for *everyone* in a Silhouette Romance, be it moms (or daughters!) or women who've found—or who still seek!—that special man in their lives. Just revel in this month's diverse offerings as we continue to celebrate Silhouette's 20th Anniversary.

It's last stop: STORKVILLE, USA, as Karen Rose Smith winds this adorable series to its dramatic conclusion. A virgin with amnesia finds shelter in the town sheriff's home, but will she find lasting love with *Her Honor-Bound Lawman*? *New York Times* bestselling author Kasey Michaels brings her delightful trilogy THE CHANDLERS REQUEST… to an end with the sparkling bachelor-auction story *Raffling Ryan*. *The Millionaire's Waitress Wife* becomes the latest of THE BRUBAKER BRIDES as Carolyn Zane's much-loved miniseries continues.

In the second installment of Donna Clayton's SINGLE DOCTOR DADS, *The Doctor's Medicine Woman* holds the key to his adoption of twin Native American boys—and to his guarded heart. *The Third Kiss* is a charmer from Leanna Wilson—a must-read pretend engagement story! And a one-night marriage that began with "The Wedding March" leads to *The Wedding Lullaby* in Melissa McClone's latest offering.…

Next month, return to Romance for more of THE BRUBAKER BRIDES and SINGLE DOCTOR DADS, as well as the newest title in Sandra Steffen's BACHELOR GULCH series!

Happy Reading!

Mary-Theresa Hussey

Mary-Theresa Hussey
Senior Editor

Please address questions and book requests to:
Silhouette Reader Service
U.S.: 3010 Walden Ave., P.O. Box 1325, Buffalo, NY 14269
Canadian: P.O. Box 609, Fort Erie, Ont. L2A 5X3

Raffling Ryan

KASEY MICHAELS

SILHOUETTE *Romance*®

Published by Silhouette Books

America's Publisher of Contemporary Romance

To Sally Hawkes, just because.

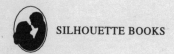 SILHOUETTE BOOKS

ISBN 0-373-19481-1

RAFFLING RYAN

Visit Silhouette at www.eHarlequin.com

Printed in U.S.A.

Books by Kasey Michaels

Silhouette Romance

Maggie's Miscellany #331
Compliments of the Groom #542
Popcorn and Kisses #572
To Marry at Christmas #616
His Chariot Awaits #701
Romeo in the Rain #743
Lion on the Prowl #808
Sydney's Folly #834
Prenuptial Agreement #898
Uncle Daddy #916
Marriage in a Suitcase #949
Timely Matrimony #1030
The Dad Next Door #1108
Carried Away #1438
 "Logan Assents"
Marrying Maddy #1469
Jessie's Expecting #1475
Raffling Ryan #1481

*The Chandlers Request...

Silhouette Yours Truly

Husbands Don't Grow on Trees

Harlequin Love & Laughter

Five's a Crowd

Silhouette Books

Baby Fever

The Fortunes of Texas
The Sheikh's Secret Son

KASEY MICHAELS,

the *New York Times* bestselling author of more than two dozen books, divides her creative time between writing contemporary romance and Regency novels. Married and the mother of four, Kasey's writing has garnered the Romance Writers of America's Golden Medallion Award and the *Romantic Times Magazine*'s Best Regency Trophy.

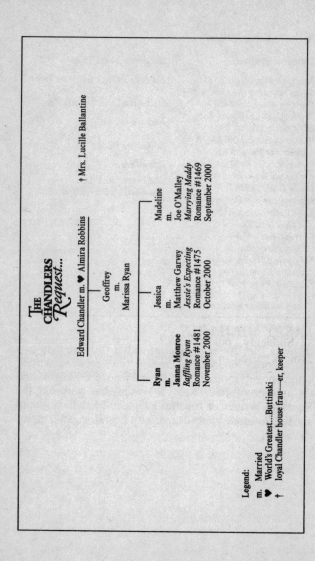

The CHANDLERS Request...

Edward Chandler m. ♥ Almira Robbins   † Mrs. Lucille Ballantine

Geoffrey
m.
Marissa Ryan

Ryan
m.
Janna Monroe
Raffling Ryan
Romance #1481
November 2000

Jessica
m.
Matthew Garvey
Jessie's Expecting
Romance #1475
October 2000

Madeline
m.
Joe O'Malley
Marrying Maddy
Romance #1469
September 2000

Legend:
m.   Married
♥   World's Greatest...Buttinski
†   loyal Chandler house frau—er, keeper

Chapter One

Almira Chandler rode along the Appalachian trails to the sound of birdsong, the wind rippling through the tall trees, and the sound of her own heavy breathing. Three miles, uphill, and then she could coast awhile, as the bike traveled downhill.

Suddenly, out of nowhere, came the sound of voices raised in near whoops. Outlaws about to attack? The end of the world? Somebody knocking on the door to announce that the long-suffering Chandler housekeeper, Mrs. Ballantine, had won some million-dollar sweepstakes?

Almira had little time to reflect, as the door to her ground-floor exercise room flew open, banging hard against the doorstop as Maddy Chandler O'Malley burst into the room, flapping her arms as if about to take flight.

Almira kept pedaling, kept her eyes on the moving screen in front of her that showed she had less than half a mile to go before she could coast. It was, after all, only Maddy. Maddy got excited when one of her roses bloomed. She went into ecstasies when her soufflés didn't fall—which they never did.

Whatever it was that Maddy had to tell her, it could wait until Almira was on the downhill side of the mountain.

Maddy skidded to a halt in front of her grandmother, waved her hands to get the woman's attention. When that failed, she did the unthinkable. She turned off the exercise video.

"That's it, kiddo, you're out of the will," Almira gasped breathlessly, her pumping legs slowing down without the incentive in front of her. Incentive like a carrot in front of a donkey, she'd always said, but it worked for her. At seventy, she needed whatever worked for her.

"This can't wait, Allie," Maddy told her. "Jessica's back from the doctor. Remember? She and Matt went today for that sonogram, ultrasound—whatever. You'll never guess. You'll never, never *ever* guess!"

Allie let go of the handlebars and checked her pulse. Calming wonderfully, right on schedule. This bike-riding stuff just might help her heart, along with her calves. Although it was her calves that concerned her, had gotten her on the bike in the first place. Not that Almira Chandler was vain.

Well, maybe just a little. There had been those cosmetic surgeries, hadn't there? But she had long ago convinced herself that if she was to keep up with her three grandchildren, she couldn't give in to age and go sit in a corner somewhere, watching soap operas.

"I'd never guess, huh?" Allie said now, stepping off the bicycle and accepting the white terry towel Maddy tossed in her direction. "Let's see. Twins?"

"*Allie!* Why are you always *doing* that?"

It had been a logical assumption, not that Allie wanted to point that out to her youngest granddaughter. She had two guesses otherwise: boy or girl. But Maddy had said she'd *never* guess. That ruled out any fifty-fifty shots. Besides, Almira was too busy being stunned, from the hot-pink terry band around her forehead, straight down to her designer sneakers. "Twins? Jessica really is carrying *twins?*"

That was what Maddy had wanted to see—her grandmother flustered. It didn't happen often, and Maddy wished she'd thought to pick up a camera and bring it into the exercise room with her. "Twins, Allie," she repeated. "Jess had to drive back here from the doctor's, because Matt seems to be in shock. Joe's with them in the other room, fanning poor Matt with the sports section of the morning paper. Oh, and neither one will tell us the sex, although they already know. That's mean."

"And Jessica?" Allie asked carefully. She knew this pregnancy hadn't been planned—had even preceded the late-July marriage ceremony by about two months. Now, in only mid-September, Jessica had been reluctantly wearing maternity clothing, moaning about her weight gain, and swearing she'd be as big as a house before she finally delivered.

Maddy dismissed her sister's reaction with a wave of her hand. "Oh, her. She's just so happy that the doctor has upped the amount of weight she can gain. In other words, she copped that last doughnut you were saving until after your ramble through the Appalachians. Ever see someone wearing powdered sugar all over a smile she can't seem to wipe off her

face? Disgusting. Come on, Allie, let's go congratu-
late them.''

Allie was already reaching for a robe, and led the
way out of the room with Maddy following close behind. "You know, Allie," Maddy said, "it's really
funny, isn't it? Jess having babies before me? I
thought I wanted them so much, and I do, but Joe
and I are having so much fun that we've decided to
wait awhile, while Jessica is happily learning how to
crochet booties. And now? Two for one? Man, am I
ever going to have some catching up to do, huh? And
Ryan. Not that anyone expects big brother ever to
marry.''

"Speak for yourself, darling," Allie said, then
pulled a ticket out of one of her pockets, handing it
to Maddy. "Here, read this."

Maddy looked over the announcement. "'Date for
a Day?''' She regarded her grandmother, then read
more. "It's for the children's wing of the hospital.
Charity event…bid on the man of your dreams who'll
do your bidding for one entire day…all proceeds go
to—*Allie!* You've signed Ryan up for this, haven't
you? Don't answer me, I can see the answer in your
eyes. Omigod! He's going to have a *cow!*''

"Nonsense, Maddy," Allie said, tying the sash of
her robe tighter around her slim waist. Almira Chandler, thanks to cosmetic surgeries and an active lifestyle, both physically and mentally, looked twenty
years younger than her seventy years…and if doing
mischief took years off a person's life, she'd look
even younger.

"I've settled you and Joe, haven't I? Settled Jessica
and Matt? Not that I'm expecting miracles, you understand, but if Ryan were just to get off his *duff,* get

out more, I'm sure he'd soon find someone *suitable*. Even better, he might find someone *unsuitable*. That's really who he needs, you know. Someone to get him out of his rut.''

Maddy was still looking at the ticket, still shaking her head. "Maximum security prison will get him out of his rut, Allie. Because he is going to *kill* you.''

''No.''

''Yes, Ryan,'' Allie countered evenly as Ryan stood up from behind his desk and began to pace.

A tall man, taller than the average, he reminded her so much of her late husband that sometimes her heart ached just looking at him. Hair as black as coal, with a tendency to wave, and with the chance of tumbling onto his forehead if only he'd let it grow past a near military shortness. His grandfather's same brilliant green eyes, sparkling with intelligence but, alas, rarely with mischief. Already thirty-three, Ryan was heading toward a settled, boring middle age.

At least he would be, if Allie left him alone, which she wasn't about to do.

He still held the ticket, and stabbed at it with the index finger of his other hand. "This—this is *ridiculous*. Auctioning off bachelors to giggly women? How much money could anything like this raise, anyway?''

''Thirty-six thousand dollars last year, I understand, with only fifty bachelors. They outfitted a whole new playroom for the in-patient children. This year there will be at least sixty, including you, darling,'' Allie slid in reasonably. ''I believe now they want to be able to hire a full-time play activities director for the unit. It's for the children, Ryan. You can't say no.''

"I can't say no because you've already signed me up!" He mashed the ticket into a ball and threw it into the wastebasket. Thanks to his high school basketball days, he had a pretty good shot, and rarely missed what he aimed at. "Okay, so I'll send a donation instead. It's a good project. But that's it. Who do I call? Who's in charge?''

"Marcia Hyatt,'' Allie mumbled, speaking into her own chest as she bowed her head. It was either that or laugh out loud, which probably would get her in trouble with her only grandson.

"Who? Marcia? Did you say *Marcia?*'' If Ryan had something else to throw, he'd have whipped it hard against the wall. "Of all the people…''

"That was years ago, Ryan, and you were never suited for each other. I certainly knew that. Besides, it would take a pretty big ego to think that she's still pining for you all these years later. And I don't think Marcia Hyatt is the pining type. Barracudas don't pine. They attack. Oh, dear. That would be unfortunate, wouldn't it? Are you sure you want to back out, darling? It might be dangerous.''

Ryan bent his head, used both hands to rub at the back of his neck. "I can't call her. She'd know I was backing out over some personal reason and, knowing her, think I was backing out in case she'd bid on me. Damn it, Allie, I'm stuck, and you know I'm stuck.''

Allie delicately coughed into her hand, covering her near purr of satisfaction. "Anyone would think I was hiring you out for hard labor in some coal mine. It's a *date,* darling. Wine and dine some woman for a single day, for a good cause. What could go wrong?''

Everything was going wrong.

From the moment Ryan showed up at Allen Country Club the night of the auction, everything had gone from bad, to worse, to damn near miserable.

Marcia had met him at the door, kissing both his cheeks as she stuck a paper badge to his tuxedo jacket touting him to be Hunk Number 22, and told him to ''Circulate, darling, circulate, and whip the ladies into a bidding frenzy. Too bad that tux doesn't show your butt. Charlie Armstrong, also on the tux list, went against the rules and wore jeans to show *his,* and a sorrier choice of attire I've never seen. Bruce Springsteen he isn't! We'll be lucky to get two hundred dollars for that idiot. But you,'' she said, patting his cheek, ''well, we're expecting some big money for you. You look so...so James Bond. I knew you would, when I added your name to the tuxedo list.''

Ryan knew he must have responded to Marcia's near monologue, but he would never be quite sure what he said as he smiled and moved away from the foyer, into the large ballroom already crowded with ''Hunks'' and their prospective bidders.

The country club had huge facilities, but the auction had been limited to the barnlike addition to the clubhouse, a huge, parquet-floored ballroom with dark, open-beamed ceilings and a stone fireplace you could roast two pigs in at the same time, with room left over for a small cow.

The chandeliers that hung from the rafters had been dimmed considerably, throwing the corners of the room into shadow and creating a more intimate atmosphere. If you were into atmosphere and, at least for tonight, Ryan most certainly was not. He was too busy reminding himself of the location of all the exits.

There were other tuxedos sprinkled throughout the crowd, he saw, as well as men dressed in casual khakis and golf shirts, some even with cardigans draped over their shoulders, the sleeves tied across their chests—a "look" Ryan had always considered too studied to be really "casual." There were men in jeans and cowboy shirts, a few in tennis whites and carrying rackets.

He even saw one guy walk by in nothing but swim trunks and thongs, a towel draped around his shoulders—and looking about as "casual" as the too deliberately casual khaki men. He also looked as if the self-adhesive paper badge pressed to his bare chest proclaiming him as Hunk Number 47 was playing hell with his few chest hairs. Which served him right, in Ryan's opinion.

Some of the men looked embarrassed. But the majority, Lord help them, seemed to be enjoying themselves very much.

Pitiful. Absolutely pitiful. He was ashamed of his own gender.

Within moments Ryan began feeling like a side of beef, as giggling women circled him, writing down his number, and then moving on. His mouth having suddenly gone as dry as a desert, he snagged a glass of wine from a passing waiter and drank it down in one gulp, then looked for a place to hide the glass, and himself, until his number was called.

As he smiled and excused himself through the crowd, he saw the temporary construction at one end of the ballroom and his knees nearly crumpled. A runway. For God's sake—a *runway*.

He couldn't believe it. He was going to have to walk down that runway? Probably while Marcia Hyatt read some drivel from a card about how rich and eligible he was.

How did Miss America contestants stand it?

"Hi. You're one of the bachelors, aren't you? I think this is where I'm supposed to say hubba-hubba, and act like some brainless twit or sex-starved career woman on the prowl for fresh meat. You won't mind if I ask you where you got that glass of wine instead, would you? I think my tongue is soon going to be stuck to the roof of my mouth."

And not a moment too soon, Ryan thought, sighing, as the near-mocking female voice finally came to a halt. Then he turned to look at the woman who'd spoken to him, surprised to see that she was taller than most women of his acquaintance, a good five feet nine in her stocking feet, he decided.

But that wasn't the only thing she didn't have in common with the women he knew, the women he occasionally dated, less frequently bedded.

For one thing, she didn't seem to have a clue as to who he was—or care, for that matter. That in itself was unusual.

And then there was the matter of her clothes. He guessed they were clothes. Either that, or she had grabbed a tablecloth off a restaurant table and wrapped it around her as a skirt on her way over here. Combined with a lemon-color ribbed sweater, her wildly flowered skirt wrapped around her like a sarong, and hung nearly to the tops of her shoes...which were brown boots. Hiking boots, it looked like.

Maybe combat boots. No. That couldn't be. Combat boots? Boots, he finally noticed, which sort of matched the brown knapsack hung over one shoulder.

Her hair was dark red as a ripe persimmon, and curled wildly around her head, framing her huge brown eyes and making her creamy white skin look even more pale. The woman wasn't even wearing lipstick, although her lips were naturally pink…and full…and looked great against her teeth as she smiled…as she was smiling now.

Whoa! Hold it! She's just different, that's all. Way different. Too different. Practically a late-night test pattern for a color television.

"I snagged this from a passing waiter," he said at last, once he'd realized he was staring. And she'd known it, he could tell from the smile on her face, the sparkle in her eyes. "If you want, I could go look for him?"

"No, that's all right. I'd really rather have a soda, anyway," she answered, then stuck out her hand. "It's Janna. Janna Monroe. And you're…?"

"Ryan Chandler," he answered, automatically taking her hand in his, surprised by the firmness of her grip. "Are you here for the auction?"

Her eyes were doing it again. Twinkling. "Yep," she said, retrieving her hand, which he had somehow forgotten to let go. "I'm here looking for a good man. Are you a good man? It's hard to tell, especially as you really look like you're hunting for the nearest way out and a quick run for the border."

Ryan smiled in spite of himself. "That obvious, huh? The truth is—" and why he was telling her the truth he'd never understand "—my grandmother set me up...*signed* me up, that is. But it is for a good cause.''

"Well, that's good. Getting roped into it is understandable. *Volunteering* to be auctioned off like a prize horse or something is...well, it's sorta *weird,* don't you think?''

Charlie Armstrong passed by at that particular moment, dressed in jeans as Marcia had said. What she hadn't said was that he was also wearing a homespun white shirt, a black leather vest, cowboy boots and a bright-white ten-gallon hat. And if that wasn't a hunk of chew ballooning out the side of his cheek, Ryan was a monkey's uncle. Especially since good old Charlie took that moment to spit into the paper cup he carried with him.

He wore the number 21 on his vest.

Charlie Armstrong was, in "real life," a pediatrician, and fifty-five if he was a day, though he looked sixty. But tonight? Tonight he was Kid Armstrong, King of the West, chewing tobacco, wearing too tight jeans, middle-aged paunch and all.

It was pitiful. And sort of funny.

Ryan looked back at Janna as Charlie sashayed through the crowd, to see her rolling her eyes and laughing in pure delight. "I don't know. Do you think I should bid on him?''

"It would be a pity bid, to hear the committee chair's opinion,'' Ryan said, then was immediately embarrassed for himself. Still, this wasn't exactly cutting up Charlie, or cutting him down. It was just a little good clean fun in the midst of a night that promised to be less than enjoyable. "He's really a good guy, you know. His wife left him two years ago, and I think he's just starting to get out and about again.''

"And doing it with a real flair," Janna added, giggling some more. "Well, I've got to move on. I'm looking over all the tall ones, you understand."

"Tall ones?" Ryan repeated, but Janna Monroe was already gone, disappearing into the crowd, although he could still see her flaming red head as she moved along. Then he shrugged. She was probably looking for the tall ones because she was tall herself. She probably wanted a man of some size, for dancing, for whatever.

Whatever?

Ryan grabbed another glass of wine from a passing waiter. What would be *whatever?*

He reluctantly went off in search of Marcia, and a list of the rules.

Ryan stood behind a portable curtain, conjuring up tortures for his grandmother. *Date for a Day?*

That might have been the original name, but Allie had forgotten to tell him that name had been changed. The auction was now dubbed *Yours for a Day,* and the possibilities that opened up to inventive minds had packed the ballroom.

There were rules, of course, and he'd found a listing of them in the foyer, on the registration table. One rule, actually. It just said that everything had to be "mutual."

Now, to define *mutual.* Mostly, to define *everything.*

He'd tell his grandmother he thought he saw a wrinkle next to her nose the next time she smiled. Yeah. That would do it. Allie would be looking in mirrors for days, trying to see that same wrinkle, and it would serve her right, considering it was her mission in life these days to do everything necessary *not* to look like anyone's soon-to-be great-grandmother.

But, for right now, all Ryan wanted to do was get out of here. Get up on the runway, listen to himself be auctioned off, and get *out of here*. He was number 22, and there were sixty-three bachelors. Did he really have to stay after his number was called?

Yeah, and like whose team of wild horses was going to keep him here?

Once the bidding started, it became pretty heated a few times, especially when the band had broken into Rod Stewart's "Da Ya Think I'm Sexy?," and Bob Rogers, one of the senior partners in the prestigious Rogers and Whitcomb Securities Inc., no less, had begun stripping off his artfully draped beige sweater and wiggling his pelvis at the women. Hit heartthrob Ricky Martin comes to Allentown, complete with banker-striped tie. Scary, that's what it was. Positively scary.

Okay, so Ryan had laughed along with everyone else, but Bob had pulled in nearly one thousand dollars for the children's wing. A person could forgive a lot of inane nonsense for one thousand bucks, right?

There had been a short intermission, during which the ladies had nibbled on small cakes and tea as they sharpened their bidding skills for the next round, and now the second bidding session was about to start.

Marcia, who had indeed taken on the role of master of ceremonies with a will—and a little more *verve* than necessary, to Ryan's mind—was counting heads behind the curtain, making sure all of the second round of bachelors had shown up. She spied Ryan, winked at him, and whispered dangerously, "You're *mine,* Chandler,'' before heading back out to the microphone; a statement that cheered Ryan not a bit.

"Good luck, Charlie!'' other bachelors called out as Charlie Armstrong's number was called and the pediatrician hiked up his jeans, tried to rearrange his paunch somewhere closer to his chest, and stepped through the opening in the curtain.

He was met by a roar of approval and the band's vocal rendition of Garth Brooks's fast-paced "Something with a Ring to It."

The crowd, as the saying goes, went wild.

And the bidding only got hotter when Charlie began singing along to the music.

"Two hundred!''

"Three-fifty!''

"Six! Six!''

"One…thousand…dollars.''

Ryan raised his eyes toward the ceiling, running that last, definitely authoritative voice through his head, processing it, and then pushed through the crowd of bachelors peeping through the curtain to take a look for himself.

He'd been right. Good Lord, he'd been right. There she was, his grandmother, standing right at the end of the runway, waving her checkbook in the air.

"Going…going…*sold,* for one thousand dollars!'' Marcia crowed from the podium, bringing down the gavel she'd probably borrowed from her father, the judge.

One thousand dollars. And Ryan was next. How was he going to top one thousand dollars?

Hell, did he *want* to?

Not really.

"Number 22!'' Marcia called out, and Ryan took

a deep breath, then stepped through the curtain. Strobe lights immediately blinded him as the room went dark except for the wildly moving colored lights that danced around the stage while the band—really pushing it now—tried their hand at the theme from *Jaws*.

Ryan fought a compulsion to turn and run for his life. Only the fact that Allie was no longer standing at the end of the runway—and making faces at him or something equally horrible—kept him going.

"Here we are, ladies, one Ryan Chandler. Tall, dark, *sinfully* gorgeous. And R-I-C-H, ladies. Oh, my goodness, yes. Could he be anything else but *extremely* talented? Ryan? Take a stroll down the runway, please, as I open the bids at…three hundred?"

The bids got to seven hundred quickly, with Ryan stiffly looking out over the crowd, his eyes concentrated on some vague point in the far distance. Marcia had the top bid, and it appeared that no one else wanted to go against the chairperson on this one— not if they wanted to be invited back next year.

And then, as Marcia was saying, "Going… going…" another voice piped up from the rear of the room. "Eight hundred!"

Marcia stopped the gavel in midslam and, with narrowed eyes, looked out into the darkness. "Eight-fifty," Marcia muttered from between clenched teeth.

"Nine," came right back at her. Closely followed by a giggle.

Ryan turned at the head of the runway, and started walking back toward Marcia. Interesting. The woman was so sleekly blond, so very controlled. And now, suddenly, her cheeks were flushed, her lips thin with anger.

He didn't know who had dared to overbid her, but whoever it was, he was certainly enjoying himself, which he just as certainly had never expected to do.

"One…thousand…dollars," Marcia said, throwing back her head, exposing the length of her throat, the height of her arrogance.

The answer came in less than a heartbeat. "One thousand five hundred. Oh, the heck with it—two thousand even!"

The crowd, which had gone silent, began murmuring, shuffling in their seats as they turned to see who was doing the bidding.

Ryan turned with them, putting a shielding hand to his forehead to try to see through the ridiculous strobe lights.

All he saw was a bright red head and a wide, happy grin as Marcia, bred never to cause a scene, brought the gavel down. "Sold! Please go to the registration desk to write your check and meet your bachelor."

Applause broke out, as Ryan had brought in the largest donation of the night thus far, and he saw Allie standing right up front again, having appeared there like a genie out of a bottle and clapping for all she was worth, giving out a few good "cowgirl" yells while she was at it.

She's enjoying *this! I'm really going to have to hurt that woman,* Ryan thought as he went back through the curtain and accepted the back-slappings and "you dog, you" congratulations of the other bachelors.

As another bachelor stepped through the curtain, this time to the strains of "Young at Heart"—a fitting song for the eighty-year-old George McDonald, chairman of the board of the hospital—Ryan made his way through the crowd in search of his grandmother.

He found her at the registration desk, having gone there right after the bidding on Ryan, she told him, in order to pay for Charlie and arrange their date.

"How...*why*...what the devil do you think you're—"

"Oh, Ryan, close your mouth," Allie scolded. "I'm not looking for romance, if that's what you think. Charlie Armstrong is the best pediatrician in town, and Jessica's babies need the best pediatrician. I'm only buttering him up, considering that I've heard he's not taking new patients right now—which will change when we're done speaking, I assure you. Besides, Charlie is taking Western line dancing lessons, and I want him to take me with him."

Ryan shook his head. "Do you ever just *do* anything, Allie? Or does everything you do have a purpose? And, that being said, are you going to let me in on the purpose behind putting me up on that runway tonight?"

Allie reached up, patted his cheek. "I just want you to have some *fun,* darling. Live a little, loosen up. Ah, and here comes your date now. Isn't she...different. Be nice, Ryan. She's probably more fragile than she looks."

"She's hardly built like a linebacker, Allie," Ryan said out of the corner of his mouth as Janna stopped, bent from the waist to untangle her skirt from her boot, showing off the limber grace of form inherent in her long-waisted, dancer-slim body.

"Yes, but that flamboyant coloring, those clothes. I think she's hiding behind them a little, Ryan, to make up for some courage she lacks. In fact, I'm will-

ing to wager she's had her heart broken at some
time." She patted his cheek again. "But you'll fix
that, won't you?"

"I'll *fix*—damn," Ryan ended. He was talking to
the air, for Allie was already back in the crowd, hanging on Charlie's arm and making the pseudocowboy
look good for it.

"Hi, again," Janna said as she walked over to
stand in front of him. "Quite the mad bidding war,
wasn't it? I was going to give up, but the auctioneer
was so *sure* she had you that I just knew I had to
rescue you. You can thank me later, unless you really
wanted to be caught in her clutches for a whole day
and evening. Besides, I was also being selfish. You're
the tallest man here."

"Tall. Yes, you mentioned that before. What does
my being tall have to do with anything?"

Janna's smile dazzled more brightly than the strobe
lights that had begun to flash again. Ryan would have
looked to the runway to see what was causing the
women to begin howling in delight, but he didn't
think he had the courage to see much more of the
auction. Not if he had to face whoever was up there
across a table at a business lunch anytime soon.

"What does it have to do with anything? Didn't
you read the rules?" she asked. "You're mine for the
day, for whatever—as long as it's legal, I'm assum-
ing. Well, I need a handyman, and you're it. And
you're tall because, even on a ladder, you have to be
tall to replace the lightbulb in the fixture over my
front door. Oh, I could do it myself, but I get sort of
dizzy up high, so I'd rather you do it. See?"

"No, no I don't see. You just paid two thousand
dollars to use *me* as a handyman for a day? You could

have hired three handymen for that price. Half a dozen.''

"True, true. But I wouldn't have this nice charity write-off, now would I? And besides, have you ever *tried* to find a handyman who just wants to do small jobs?'' She threw back her head, showing her own long neck, and it was longer, and whiter, than Marcia's. "Lots of luck, that's what I say, trying to find a man like that.'' She grinned. "So I bought you.''

"Because I'm tall. Because I can reach the light fixture over your front door. That's it? That's your *reason?*''

She stuck out one leg, and her rather adorable chin, and braced one hand on her hip. "No,'' she said, her smile gone. "I picked you because of those killer bedroom eyes of yours. I took one look and wanted to jump your bones, big boy. There, happy now?''

Ryan had the grace to look ashamed, even feel ashamed. "You really do want me to be your handyman for the day. I—I'm sorry I didn't understand from the first.''

"That's all right,'' Janna said, patting his shoulder, the way he imagined she'd pat a puppy who'd just got nervous on her carpet. She handed him a piece of paper. "Here. This is my address. According to The Weather Channel—if you're into wild prognostications—this Saturday is going to be a lovely Indian summer kind of day. Perfect for handyman jobs. Be there at 8:00 a.m., okay? Now, I've gotta go see someone about a check.''

He pointed toward the registration desk. "You're going the wrong way. You pay over there,'' he told her, still trying to figure out what had just happened to him. Was he happy to have been rescued from

Marcia? Or had he just been tossed from the frying pan straight into the fire, as the old saying went?

Janna grimaced, looking as comical as a pretty woman could, which, in her case, was pretty comical. Rather like watching a young Lucille Ball coming down the stairs in a ball gown, then looking into the camera lens and deliberately crossing her eyes. He had to smile, in spite of himself. "I know. But first I have to see…I have to…well, don't you worry about me. I'll see you Saturday morning."

And then she was gone, and Ryan was standing there, holding the note, written, it appeared, in dark-brown eyebrow pencil: "Janna Monroe. 540 Washington Avenue. Eight o'clock. Be there or be square."

Chapter Two

Janna stood at the kitchen sink, looking out the window at the sun as it rose slowly in the sky. It was Saturday, the sun was shining, and The Weather Channel had been right on target, because the expected high today was seventy-two degrees.

She glanced at the clock on the wall above the cabinets, watching for a moment as the turquoise-blue plastic cat wagged its tail as each second passed, bringing the time closer to eight o'clock. The cat's big yellow eyes also moved with the second hand, shifting side to side in true feline fashion, and she grinned at it, thinking it was grinning at her, anticipating an interesting day.

Tansy, her real-life blue-cream shorthaired cat and boon companion since she'd rescued the then small, fuzzy kitten from the animal shelter eight months earlier, politely rubbed up against her jean-covered leg, reminding Janna that she hadn't been fed yet. ''Always the lady, Tansy. Good for you. I'll be with you in a minute.''

The cat looked up at her hopefully, then hopped onto the counter without seeming to move at all. She was just on the floor one moment, and standing next to the soapy water-filled sink the next. Tilting her head to one side, Tansy began to ''talk'' to Janna.

And she really did talk, Tansy did. Just because nobody understood her didn't mean she didn't talk, or so Janna had explained to Zachary when her son teased her for talking back to a cat.

''Yes, yes,'' Janna said, ''I'm washing your dishes now. Yes,'' she continued after Tansy held up her end of the conversation, ''the pink one with the flowers on it. I know it's your favorite.''

Seemingly satisfied with that answer, Tansy began her premeal ablutions, licking her front paw and then rubbing it over her whiskered face.

Janna shook her head. ''I really should get out more,'' she said, not to Tansy but to herself. ''Next thing you know, I'll be talking to the clock, too.''

Her musings were interrupted by Zachary's footsteps thundering down the hallway. He slid into the kitchen, stopping precisely next to his chair at the table. ''Hi, Mom,'' the nine-year-old said as he picked up the granola bar Janna had laid there for him. ''Bye, Mom,'' he continued around his first mouthful, already heading for the door.

''I don't think so,'' Janna said, rinsing Tansy's dish under the tap and placing it in the dish drainer. ''Haven't you forgotten something?''

Zachary, a brown-eyed, red-haired, freckle-faced miniature of his mother, screwed up his face in thought. ''Oh, yeah, right. I'll be over at Tommy's.

We've got soccer practice at ten, remember? We've got to practice.''

"You've got to practice for the practice," Janna said, nodding. "Understandable. Now, what else have you forgotten?"

Zachary comically screwed up his face once more, concentrating. "Nope. Can't think of anything," he said, trying not to smile.

"Now you've done it," Janna said, advancing on him as he retreated toward the back door. She grabbed his face with her wet, soapy hands and planted a big, fat kiss on his forehead, then rubbed soapsuds into his cheeks, just for the fun of it.

"Aw, Mom," Zachary complained, but his heart wasn't in it. He was in too much of a hurry to run past her and scoop up some soap bubbles of his own. Once armed with two near mountains of bubbles, he advanced on Janna, *heh-heh-hehing* like the evil landlord about to toss poor, defenseless Little Nell out into the blizzard.

Janna rapidly retreated, looking for weapons as she went. Nothing. Not close enough to the refrigerator to get the canned whipped cream; too far away from the sink to reload there.

There was nothing else to do but make a break for it. Still watching Zachary, she struggled to open the back door, her slippery hands not making much progress on the doorknob.

Emitting *eeks* and *acks* and various other exclamations meant to show her "terror," she finally wrenched the door open, then sidestepped quickly as Zachary, hot on her tail, couldn't stop himself from running straight outside…and smack into the man standing on the back stoop, holding up his hand as if ready to knock on the door.

The two small mountains of soap bubbles became a casualty of the collision, some of them slamming into Ryan Chandler's chest, some of them flying up and finding new homes in Zachary's hair, on Ryan's nose.

Ryan's hands came down on Zachary's shoulders to steady him, and he looked past the boy to the mother, who was leaning against the back door, laughing, and not trying to be quiet about it, either. Her laugh rang out pure and full and with genuine enjoyment, even as she pushed herself away from the door and grabbed a dish towel, handing it to Ryan. "Hi, Mr. Chandler," she said. "You and Zachary have already bumped into each other, I see. Do come in."

"Gotta go, Mom," Zachary said, wiping his hands on his sweatpants. "Tommy's mother drives today, so I'll be home around lunchtime, okay? See you, um, Mr. Chandler. Oh, and sorry about that."

With that, Zachary was off, racing across the back-yard to his friend, and Janna didn't bother to stop him. After all, he had apologized, hadn't he?

"I didn't know you had a son," Ryan said, handing back the dish towel as he entered the house behind Janna and looked around the kitchen, pretty much as if he'd never seen one before today.

Janna looked around with him. She really loved her kitchen. It was the one room in the house where she had definitely let herself go, indulging her love of color as well as cramming every available space with one of her first loves: gadgets.

The kitchen set was a genuine antique, a sort of

Art Deco chrome-legged set with Formica top—a turquoise Formica top, with matching padded chairs. She'd seen a set much like it at a local furniture store, new, and had laughed to think that her grandmother's cast-off set from the fifties had stuck around long enough to show up in decorating reruns.

The walls were also turquoise, bright against the high old, glass-fronted cabinets she'd covered with not one but six careful layers of white paint and decorated with chrome pulls and handles in the shape of pineapples.

Then there was the bright-white tile floor she'd laid herself, with turquoise, pink and yellow tiles scattered throughout, ruffled curtains of turquoise, pink and yellow stripes she'd patched together out of remnants, the colorful prints on the walls, the dozen or so birdhouses and green, trailing plants in the space between the cabinets and the ceiling, the turquoise Formica countertops covered with bread maker, toaster oven, can opener, blender, pasta maker and several other can't-live-without-it gadgets and…well…it was a "full" kitchen. No doubt.

One might even call it cluttered. To look at Ryan Chandler, he was one of those who definitely would.

"Would you like a cup of coffee before you get started?" she asked, drying off her hands and setting the flowered bowl on the floor, filling it with dry cat food. "Of course you do. You sit down over there while I get it. Oh, and the list is on the table."

When she turned away from the coffeepot to approach the table holding two stoneware cups, one pink, one turquoise, Ryan was staring at her. In fact, she got the feeling that he had done nothing but stare at her since his first inspection of the room.

She looked down at herself, and saw nothing out of the ordinary. She was wearing jeans. Okay, old jeans. Okay, *very* old jeans. Very old, soft, and somewhat *tight* jeans, worn low on her hips and hugging her very long legs.

What else would she wear if she and Ryan were going to be working on odd jobs all day? Well, a knit sweater, for one thing. And she was wearing one. A dark-gray sweater-vest once belonging to her late husband—which had shrunk badly in the wash—that she sometimes wore with a blouse, and sometimes without.

She looked down at herself again. Okay, so she should probably have worn a blouse under it today.

And maybe a bra.

She winced as she looked at herself.

Definitely a bra. *I mean,* she thought, *how was I to know the guy would turn catatonic on me, for crying out loud? They're just nipples. Everybody's got them. He's got them, for crying out loud.*

Okay, and so maybe her venerable, shrunken sweater also didn't quite *meet* the waistband of her jeans. Hadn't the man ever seen a belly button before, either?

Still…did she look that bad, that terrible? She had pulled her thick, long, unruly mop of redder than red hair up on top of her head, securing it there with a rubber band, so that curls tumbled all over the place— back, front, sides. She always thought she looked like a really, really big chrysanthemum when she wore her hair this way, but it was comfortable, and it kept the mop out of her eyes and…*"What?"* she exclaimed at last, exasperated, and nearly spilling the coffee. "Why are you *looking* at me like that?"

"I haven't the faintest idea," Ryan answered her, taking one of the cups from her and sipping its contents, his gaze now carefully lowered. "What's this?" he said before taking another sip. "It's coffee, yes, but there's something else...."

"They're French vanilla coffee beans, with a dash of apple cinnamon strudel flavor tossed in," she told him, sitting down across the table from him. "Like it?"

"First thing in the morning? No. But, since I've already had two cups at home, yes, it tastes pretty good. Some special blend?"

"I pick it up at the mall, actually. There's a gourmet coffee kiosk on the upper level. Every time we're at the mall, I pick up another flavor. I've got a Jamaican blend that would put hair on your fingernails, I swear, but I didn't think you'd like it. So," she said, putting down her cup and bracing her elbows on the table, "what do you want to do first?"

His smile did something very strange, setting off a small explosion somewhere in the pit of her stomach. "Do first? Frankly, I'd like to offer you your money back and the services of a first-class handyman. But somehow I don't think you'd go for that. Or would you?"

She pretended to consider this for a moment, then shook her head, her mop of curls speaking quite eloquently as they bobbed back and forth. "Nope. No deal. We have a bargain, right?"

She'd stick to that answer: a bargain. She wouldn't mention anything else, couldn't mention anything else. Not when she didn't really understand it herself. She only knew she was doing a nice old lady a favor, and she would never renege on her promise.

Especially when her To-Do list was nearly as long as one of Ryan Chandler's long arms.

Janna picked up the paper, scanned it. "I think you should start with the garage. Zach thinks it's his private dumping grounds, but I need more storage space for my own stuff. I bought some shelving—you can put shelving together, can't you?—and after you take everything out of the garage and hose down the floor, we can get everything arranged. Oh, and I'll help put the shelves together, I promise."

He looked at her as if she had just told him to climb to the top of Mount Everest and bring her back a tutti-frutti flavored icicle. "You're kidding, right?"

She looked back at him blankly. "Kidding? Nope. Why would I be kidding?"

He reached up, scratched at a spot behind his left ear. "I don't know," he said. "Maybe I thought you'd want to go for a drive, have lunch at some country inn, maybe take in dinner later? Dancing? You know, the sort of thing every other bachelor is probably doing this weekend with the women who bid on them. But clean a garage? Put up shelves?"

"Put *together* shelves, then put them *up*. There's a difference. These are just inexpensive metal thingies, freestanding shelves we sort of smash back against the walls to load my junk onto." She rolled her eyes at him. "I mean, I wouldn't ask you to put together *real* shelves. We have too much else to do to fool with something like *that*."

Now he rubbed a hand across his jaw. He really was quite expressive with his hand movements, although he probably didn't know that. "Got any aspirin, Ms. Monroe?" he asked after a moment.

She got up quickly to get the aspirin bottle down

from the cabinet, keeping her eyes on him. Look how he frowned. He was so cute when he frowned. Tall, dark, green-eyed…and really, really cute. Almost cuddly, although she doubted anyone had ever told *him* that! She nearly dropped the aspirin bottle, realizing that her mind had taken a quantum leap from dirty garages to…well, she'd think about all of that later, wouldn't she? "You have a headache?" she asked.

"No, but I'm pretty sure I will any minute now," Ryan said, accepting the two tablets she handed him, swallowing them down with a sip of coffee, and then heading for the back door.

Janna felt the sudden, irresistible need to make a stupid fool of herself, something she could usually do with quite a flourish, especially considering she hadn't felt foolish about a man—especially a man like Ryan Chandler—in a very, very long time.

"The garage door has one of those electronic openers," she told him, hands on hips as she felt her tongue begin to run on wheels. "The code is 0000, as it's easy to remember—and because zero is the lowest number on the keypad and Zachary could reach it by the time he was five and we put it up—and then you press the Enter button and the door goes right up. Sorry if I'm rattling on. I was just giving you a bit of Monroe folklore, or whatever. You don't mind, do you? No, of course you don't."

"Uh-huh," he said, shaking his head as he pulled the door shut behind him.

Janna put her hands on her hips and stared at the closed door for some moments. The colorful room suddenly seemed drab, now that he'd left it. "The man's obviously in a daze," she told herself with false concern and a pot full of ulterior motive. "He'll forget the code on his own," she said out loud finally, and went after him.

Three hours, four bandages, and several muttered curse words later, the garage was clean. Hell, it sparkled, if a garage could be said to sparkle.

And, much to Ryan's surprise, he was beginning to enjoy himself.

Janna had been as good as her word, and had helped screw together the inexpensive, freestanding metal shelves, using an electric screwdriver that had enough attachments to be standard issue on a manned Mars landing-and-recovery module.

As she had put the last bandage on his scraped elbow, a maneuver he couldn't quite manage himself, she'd kissed the cartoon-covered strip to "make it all better."

He hadn't even felt insulted, being lumped into Zachary's age group, where kissing to make things better must be standard operating procedure.

Besides, it worked.

"Where to now, boss?" he asked, still feeling pretty good about himself. He was, after all, in very good shape. He worked out three times a week in his own home exercise room—without resorting to Allie's motivational exercise tapes. He golfed. He played the occasional game of tennis—although never against Allie, who cheated blatantly. "Out" to his grandmother only counted if *she* called it.

"Where to now? Upstairs, to the main bathroom," Janna answered, already leading the way.

The trip to the second floor meant that Ryan was going to get a look at her house, which intrigued him mightily. Outside, it was a typical redbrick Cape Cod, although the bright-yellow shutters and woodwork were, to say the least, out of the ordinary. However, once inside her kitchen, he'd known that here lived a woman who was either color blind or in love with color. Bright colors. Sunshiny colors. Happy colors. She'd even painted the interior of her garage a sunny yellow—with blue stripes, no less.

They passed through the kitchen and directly into the dining room. Ryan stopped in his tracks, instantly mesmerized by the hand-painted mural on the wall shared with the kitchen. It was a scene from a park, a Paris park, in fact. He recognized snippets from his art history classes. The tree in the foreground. The lady in the hat, exposing her profile and the bustle of her long skirt.

"Isn't that Monet?" he asked, pointing to the mural.

Her grin flashed at him, once again nearly blinding him—he'd really have to get used to the fact that she seemed so damned *happy* all the time. "Nope. It's a Monroe," she corrected, idly tracing a finger over the lady's profile. "See? That's me under the hat. And the little boy? That's Zachary, although he was only five then, of course. Oh, it might have started out as a Monet, but I added a few touches of my own. Like the parrot in that tree over there. Like it?"

Ignoring the parrot, Ryan peered closely at the woman's face. Damn if it wasn't Janna Monroe, complete with burnished curls. He slowly shook his head. "Remarkable. You're quite good, you know. A little flaky, maybe, but good."

"I'll take that as a compliment. The little bit flaky

part, especially. Mark, my husband, said being flaky was my most endearing trait.''

"Your husband," Ryan repeated, surprised to feel so shocked to learn about this man called Mark. Maybe he had thought Zachary had been hatched under a cabbage patch. Maybe he'd thought she'd had a youthful fling. But a husband? Why hadn't he considered the fact that she might have—or had—a husband?

"Mark, yes," Janna said evenly. "He's not in the mural because I couldn't…well, I couldn't bring myself to paint his portrait after he died. That was when Zachary was eighteen months old, a few years before we moved here from Soho, in fact. Shall we go upstairs now?''

Ryan followed her to the center hall and the stairs, only vaguely taking in the old but comfortable-looking faded chintz couches in the living room, the round oak pedestal table that sat in the dining room. It was the furniture of castoffs, of well-loved hand-me-downs. The sort of things found in a first apartment, or a newlyweds' home. And, he thought fleetingly, not the sort of home or furniture that cried out that Janna Monroe had an extra two thousand dollars lying around to fling at a charity, any charity. "Soho? You lived in New York City?''

"We had a loft," she told him, climbing the stairs ahead of him, giving him a good view of her jean-covered rear. Ryan deliberately looked away. He was much too enthralled with the view not to look away. "Mark was an artist, and quite good. Sculptor, actually. Much better than me. A couple of his works are in parks in New Jersey and Connecticut. But there was no sense staying, not after he was gone, and we'd always wanted Zachary to grow up with grass and trees and Little League. So I finally decided to leave, closed my eyes and stabbed a finger on the map, and we moved here."

"What if you had ended up with your finger stuck in the middle of Lake Erie, or even the Atlantic Ocean?" Ryan asked, wondering if, just maybe, he'd fallen down a rabbit hole and was now doing his version of *Alice's Adventures in Wonderland.* The gray-blue-and-orange-mottled feline perched at the top of the steps didn't look like the Cheshire Cat, but the thing *was* grinning at him, damn it.

Janna turned at the top of the stairs, looking back at him. "Oh, that wouldn't have happened," she told him.

"Why not?" he asked. Then the word that had been chanting in his head off and on for the past two hours chimed out again: *hippie.* Was it possible Janna was a neo-hippie, if there were such things as neo-hippies, considering most of the real hippies were soon going to be old enough to apply for retirement benefits from the Establishment they'd vowed never to trust. Still, he gave it a shot. "Or do you think it was your karma or something?"

"Karma? Gee, I haven't heard that one in a while," she said, turning to lead the way toward the bathroom. "No, it wouldn't happen because I researched several cities carefully, checked out schools and crime levels and all that stuff, made my choice, then peeked before I poked. But don't tell Zachary. He thinks I'm brilliant. Besides, it pays to have children believe their parents just might have special powers, or eyes in the backs of their heads. At least until they're old enough to know better than to touch matches or play with unknown dogs, or take candy from strangers. Right now, I'm omnipotent to Zachary, and he believes everything that comes out of my mouth. Believes and obeys. And that's the way I'm going to keep it, at least until he's heading for college.''

"How old is he? Nine? Ten?"

"Nine and three-quarters," Janna told him, pulling a face. "I'm running out of time, aren't I? I mean, last week he asked me how he got here." She rolled her eyes. "I told him, of course, as you should always answer serious questions truthfully, but I didn't say much—no more than he'd asked. But I won't say it isn't hard for a mother and son, especially in situations like that. There are times when I miss Mark so much...."

Then she grinned again, her eyes coming alive once more. "Here we are. How good are you with a caulk gun?"

Ryan didn't answer for a moment. He was too busy thinking about what Allie had said. What was it? Oh, yes, something about Janna Monroe putting on those bright colors and happy smiles to hide something sad inside her. How he hated when his grandmother was right.

And then there was the fact that he had, without really noticing, somehow walked down the hallway and straight into what could only be Janna's bedroom.

This room, compared to the other rooms he had seen, seemed plain, almost stark. A virgin room, with a single bed, and no sign of color or froufrou lace he'd come to expect in a woman's bedroom.

For all the verve, the color, the absolute *joy* of the rest of the house, this room could have been plucked straight from an eighteenth-century nunnery.

Yes, Ryan told himself. This was a woman who held a few secret sorrows. A widow with a son and a lot of memories she was either trying to banish or hold to herself, cling to by not surrounding herself with womanly things, loverlike things.

"Ryan—yoo-hoo? Caulk guns? Are you familiar with them?"

He looked at the thing Janna was now waving in front of his face. Big. Gray metal. Sort of like a gun, but not like a gun. And totally incomprehensible to him as to how the thing could and should be used.

He gently pushed the caulk gun to one side, so that it was no longer pointed at him, even if it wasn't loaded. "My mother never allowed me to play with guns," he said, hoping a little levity—no matter how bad—might defuse this potentially embarrassing situation.

"You don't know, do you?" Janna asked, but he could tell that it was a rhetorical question, so he didn't answer. "Do you want to learn?"

"Why don't you ask me if I want a root canal? That answer might be yes, as it seems more painless. What do you *do* with that thing?"

Janna proceeded to demonstrate, loading a container of caulk into the gun and then motioning for Ryan to follow her into the bathroom.

"Gun, tub. Caulk, crack. Aim, fire," she said, each word punctuated by hand movements that certainly brought her point across, but that did nothing to make Ryan feel as if she were Tom Sawyer and he should now be looking longingly at a pail of whitewash and a mile of fence.

"You're kidding, right?"

Janna tipped back an imaginary cowboy hat with

the plastic tip of the caulk insert, then rubbed a hand under her nose as she leaned against the shower stall. "Whatsa matter, bucko? You chicken? Here," she declared, all but throwing the caulk gun into his hands. "I'll even hum the theme from *High Noon,* if that will help."

Chicken? How dare she...how dare she *laugh* at him! And look so damn cute while she did it, which only made him angrier than he'd been, and he had been getting pretty peeved at this whole idea. Cleaning a garage was one thing. Not a great thing, but he had felt some stupid sense of accomplishment once the chore had been completed. But to be dared— pretty close to *double*-dared—into getting down on his hands and knees inside a cramped shower stall and shooting *gunk* into the cracks between the bright-pink tiles?

Not in this lifetime, he wasn't!

Yes, he was. Because she *had* dared him, and the twinkle in her huge brown eyes told him she already knew she'd won.

Janna stepped past him, back into the hall. "I don't think I can watch this. I'll be downstairs, starting the grill for lunch. You do like charbroiled hamburgers, don't you?"

"If I said I was hypoglycemic and needed red meat now, would you let me start the grill and kill the shower stall after lunch?"

Janna tipped her head to one side, considering his offer. "You're not, are you? Really hypoglycemic, that is? No, of course you're not. But I have to hand it to you, that was a good excuse. Just don't ever repeat it around Zach, okay?"

"So I get to start the fire?" Ryan asked, wondering

if he sounded as pathetic as he felt. Here he was, a grown man, and he hadn't the faintest idea how to do a simple household repair. But then, why should he? He'd been born with the proverbial silver spoon in his mouth, and had never done any more onerous chores than making up his own bed. He didn't know if he could justify his lack of mechanical skills, or if he was just plain embarrassed by that lack.

Either way, he figured starting a gas grill won hands down over caulking tub tile.

"Tell you what. You start the fire and I'll caulk the tiles. Deal?" Janna said, and if she was laughing at him or rescuing him he didn't know. He just knew he felt a sudden urge to grab her up, kiss her senseless for her compassion.

Still, like a man fighting over a lunch check, he did the polite thing and responded, "No, no. There's no need. I can fix the tile after lunch. Really."

"Really?" Janna shot right back at him. "Now, is it my turn to say you shouldn't be silly, that I'll do it? Because if it is, you're plain out of luck, bucko, because you're on. You can do the job after lunch." She put down the caulk gun, laying it carefully on a plush rug with a huge pink rose sort of blossoming in the middle of it. "I'm feeling filthy after wading through the dirt in the garage. I think I'll just go take a shower in the other bathroom, then come downstairs when I smell the burgers cooking."

Ryan watched her go, tried very hard not to imagine her in the shower. Her wet skin glistening. One of those weird "net" things all soapy as she ran it over her skin.

Down her arm. Across her legs.

Bending to soap her leg.

He closed his eyes tight, tried to banish the image.
Shame, shame, shame on him.

Go downstairs and light the fire? He wouldn't even
have to turn on the propane. Hell, all he'd have to do
was *look* at the coals and they'd ignite!

Chapter Three

Ryan was still muttering under his breath as he slammed out of the kitchen door and onto the small brick patio. Outfoxed by a woman. Outmaneuvered by a woman who knew darn full well she'd just scored and he'd lost.

He knew that because she laughed—giggled, even—all the way back down the hall, until she turned into the second door on the left, which housed the main bathroom.

Before he'd gotten halfway down the stairs he'd heard the shower turn on, and before he could make himself walk past the dining room mural that still drew him like a magnet, she was singing at the top of her lungs.

She was taking a shower, getting clean. How nice for her.

While he was hot, sweaty, dirty and felt pretty much like he'd been hired out to be on a chain gang. Oppressed. Overworked. Definitely not appreciated.

And, unfortunately, not very well equipped to look good while he was mucking around doing ridiculous chores the rest of the male world could probably complete with one hand tied behind their backs.

He had a huge pull in the front of his brand-new designer shirt, a cartoon bandage on his elbow, smears of dirt all over his khaki slacks and...as he passed by a small mirror in the hall...it would seem that he'd somehow gotten something *green* stuck in his hair that Janna hadn't bothered to mention to him.

Yeah. A root canal probably would be more fun.

He could cheerfully strangle the woman, and lay the blame squarely where it belonged—on Allie. There wasn't a jury in the country that would convict him.

What really bothered him, and what he really wished he wouldn't be considering, or worrying about, was what a really rotten impression he must be making on Janna Monroe.

Not that he liked her. How could anyone like such an obvious...an obvious—was she really a *flake?* Could he honestly call her that?

No. No, he couldn't. She was a widow with a son. She had her own business, although he still didn't know what that was. He only knew it took reams of paper to run that business, and he knew because he'd loaded about a ton's worth onto the new shelves in the garage.

She owned a home. She seemed to be a good mother. She knew how to use a caulk gun....

"Damn her," Ryan said, his heart not in his words enough to raise them much above a whisper. Still, the child heard him.

He hadn't heard the child, probably because he

wasn't looking at anything besides the old-fashioned barbecue grill he'd just uncovered. He'd planned on turning a switch and starting a propane gas grill. But there was no propane tank. There wasn't even very much of a grill, just an ancient big kettle on three legs, a bag of charcoal stored under the hood, and some liquid fire starter and long matches.

At least he wouldn't have to rub two sticks together.

"You're mad at Mom?" the voice behind Ryan asked, so that he whirled around, the box of matches flying from his hand and opening, spilling all over the bricks. "What'd she do?"

Ryan bit down on yet another "damn," knowing that little pitchers have big ears, or whatever it was Mrs. Ballantine had said the day her young grandnephew had visited the household and Allie had plucked a few choice words from her vocabulary when the kid had put his foot through her new tennis racket.

"Hi," he said instead, plastering a wide smile on his face. After that, he was lost, because he'd never been around children much at all, and worried he might not be good with them.

Zachary seemed to sense this, and tipped his head at him the same infuriating way his mother had done earlier, then said, "You don't know how to light the grill, do you? Want me to do it?"

"Aren't you supposed to be somewhere else?" Ryan nearly growled. What had happened to him this morning? Had he suddenly turned transparent, his every flaw, his every lack, able to be seen?

"I would still be at practice, except that Timmy Wetherhold took a header straight into the goal and

Coach had to take him to the emergency room. Man, was he ever *bloody*. It was cool. So, what's for lunch?''

Bloodthirsty little savage, Ryan thought, then remembered his own youth, and how cool he had thought it the day Parker Soames had run into a lacrosse bat and nearly sliced off his ear. Parker had been fine, but definitely bloody, and Ryan, at the ripe old age of thirteen, still hadn't figured out that injuries could be serious. That was a good time in life, when a kid believed himself and everyone else to be immortal.

It had been, now that he thought back on it, only about three years before his parents died in that plane crash.

After that, he had understood mortality, and his world had considerably sobered as he'd felt the need to grow up overnight.

He wondered why Zach didn't feel that way, after losing his father. He was younger than Ryan had been, granted, but life hadn't exactly been kind to the kid. And yet he was just that—a kid. A happy, extroverted, pretty cool kid.

Janna Monroe must be doing something right.

Zachary helped Ryan pick up the matches—it was a large, economy-size box, and nearly full—still talking about Timmy Wetherhold and his injury. "Coach says he'll be fine, that wounds to the head bleed a lot, and since Timmy started screeching the minute he hit, we know he didn't go all unconscious or anything dangerous. But he'll need stitches, which seemed to cheer him up a lot. Here you go," he ended, handing the last of the matches to Ryan. "Why don't you get the hamburger out of the refrigerator and patty it out while I start the fire? I can do it, honest.''

Great. Now he was being condescended to by a nine-and-three-quarters-year-old. Condescended to, and probably fibbed to, in the bargain. ''Your mother lets you light the grill? Now, why don't I believe that?''

Zach ran a hand through his mop of red hair. ''I said I *could* do it,'' he said, making a face. ''I never said I've *done* it. But I can. I've watched Mom a million times.''

''Then this will make one million and one, because you're going to watch me, okay?'' Ryan said, winking at the boy, beginning to relax around him. Talking to boys wasn't so bad. They were, after all, the same species. Even the same sex, if not the same generation. How much could boys change since he'd been a kid?

''Okay, sure,'' Zachary agreed, plopping himself down in a nearby chair. ''Just yell if you run into trouble.''

''Wise guy,'' Ryan grumbled under his breath, although he couldn't help smiling. ''How about we do it together? Will that make you happy?''

Zachary was out of the chair like a bullet shot out of a gun, grabbing some newspaper from a small stack on the shelf between the grill legs. ''We need this to help get the coals started,'' he explained as he lifted the metal grid and shoved some pages of scrunched-up paper in the kettle base. ''Now you pour on some charcoal. Not too much, because we're only having hamburgers.''

Ryan did as he was told, carefully pouring from the large blue-and-white bag, then using his already dirty

fingers to arrange the charcoal evenly. He went to put
the metal grid back on top, but Zachary stopped him.

"You want to squirt some of that fire starter stuff
on first. If you do it with the grill on top, the hamburgers can taste sorta funny."

"I knew that," Ryan said quickly, lying through
his teeth. That lie made it impossible for him to read
the instructions on the side of the can, which he
wanted to do, so he just flipped the plastic top and
squirted liquid onto the coals, then picked up the
matches.

"Not yet," Zachary warned him. The kid was beginning to really get on Ryan's nerves. "Mom says
to wait until the stuff soaks in a while, so it doesn't
just burn off and the coals don't light. But you knew
that, too, right? Mom says to never lie, because you'll
only trip yourself up somewhere and then everyone
will know. So you wouldn't lie to me, because you're
a grown-up, and you already know what Mom said."

"Did *Mom* ever think about sending you away to
military school?" Ryan asked, putting the matches
down again. Just what he needed. He was spending
the day playing very unhandy handyman, and now he
was getting lessons in fire starting, and life, from a
freckle-faced kid. It was true. There just wasn't any
justice in this world.

"Nope. Is that what you did, Mr. Chandler? Go
away to school? That must have been the pits."

"It wasn't so bad," Ryan said, remembering his
days at private school. He'd been fairly popular, good
at sports, and when he picked up a basketball and
showed a talent for the game that was definitely out
of the ordinary, well, life had gotten pretty good for
a while. "You can make a lot of very good friends

at school, especially when you know you have to depend on each other for company.''

"Yeah? Well don't tell Mom. She thinks private schools are for kids whose parents don't want them around. And she wants me to have a diversified education—I think that's what she calls it. You know, meeting lots of different people from different backgrounds and stuff. Mom's got all these ideas, you know. Some of them are a little screwy, but most of them are good. You can light the fire now.''

"Huh?" Ryan shook his head, slow to follow up on Zachary's quick change of subject. Maybe kids from this new generation *were* different. He certainly didn't remember being quite so grown-up when he was nine and three-quarters. "You trust me to do this?" he asked Zachary.

The boy looked consideringly at the grill, then at Ryan. "I think you can handle it," he said, and then he grinned. "I mean, we've done everything Mom does, I think. So go ahead.''

"Thank you," Ryan said, tongue-in-cheek, and struck a match, tossing it onto the coals.

The fire began slowly, the paper beneath the coals catching first, then feeding up to the coals. But that was as far as the fire got before turning into nothing more than some smoke and a little "graying" of a few coals.

Ryan looked at his failure for a few moments, then gritted his teeth and picked up the fire starter. He'd be damned if he'd let this simple task beat him; not when he already knew he'd be a bust at caulking around the tile.

"You're not going to squirt more on, are you?" Zachary asked. "I don't think you should do that.''

"Oh, really. You want peanut-butter-and-jelly sandwiches for lunch?"

"You're getting testy, aren't you? That's what Mom says. That men get testy sometimes, especially when things don't go their way."

"Your mom ought to write a book," Ryan said, squirting the fire with enough starter to drown it into a heavily smoking mass that nearly obliterated the grill entirely.

There was only one way to shut off the ever growing column of smoke, and that was to turn it into fire. So thinking, Ryan struck another match and tossed it in the general direction of the kettle.

It worked.

Boy, did it work.

The smoke was gone in an instant, replaced by a *whoosh* of flame that shot a good six feet into the air…and caught hold on the canvas awning hanging over the kitchen window.

"Oh, *wow!*" Zachary exclaimed as Ryan reacted by grabbing the child around the waist and running him off the porch. "Now I remember what I forgot. I forgot to tell you to move the kettle out from under the window!"

The boy shouldn't have had to tell Ryan that last little bit of information. He should have known it on his own, damn it. Any idiot would know not to light a fire right under a very flammable piece of material.

Any idiot but Ryan Chandler, that is.

"Stand here. Stand right here!" he yelled to Zachary, who obeyed without question. Ryan picked up a long wooden picnic bench and returned to the patio, using the bench as a sort of battering ram with which he pushed over the kettle, so that the wildly burning coals spilled onto the grass, where they could do no more damage.

Besides, the damage had already been done. The canvas awning wasn't just smoldering. It had sort of ''popped'' into full flame, and the open window had created enough draft that the kitchen curtains were also on fire.

''The hose! Where's the hose?'' he yelled, running back to Zachary.

Zachary, his eyes wide as saucers as he watched the flames, mutely pointed to the corner of the house, and the coiled hose that lay there, attached to an outside faucet.

Ryan turned on the water, handed the hose to Zachary, and then ran inside the house, covering his mouth with the collar of his shirt as he ran upstairs...to be met by Janna, who was running downstairs.

Wrapped in a towel.

''Do I smell smoke?'' she asked, her red curls dripping wet, as was the rest of her. ''I do, don't I? What did you do?''

''Just get outside with Zachary,'' Ryan ordered, pulling her toward the front of the house. The back of the house, the part housing the kitchen, was a more direct route, but he didn't want her to see the flames, panic...or maybe kill him. ''I'll call the fire department.''

''You haven't called the— Ohmigod! Where's Zachary?''

By now they were running around the side of the house, heading for the patio, and Ryan found himself somehow caught between trying to dial 911 on his cell phone and wondering how tightly Janna had tucked the bath towel that covered her from breasts to thighs.

Clearly, he didn't have too strong a grasp on his sanity at the moment.

Zachary, however, was coming on like gangbusters, the hose firmly directed at the open kitchen window as flames continued to grow inside the house.

Janna grabbed the hose from him and called out to Ryan that there was a fire extinguisher in the kitchen, under the sink—and could he please try to get it.

"Right," he answered, wondering when he had begun harboring this death wish, and lifted his shirt to cover his mouth once more, then ran inside the kitchen.

Between the hose and the extinguisher, the fire was actually out by the time the fire department arrived on the scene.

Ryan decided to think about this as a good thing. It sure beat the hell out of thinking about how the fire had *started,* which was through his own carelessness...along with his stupid notion of proving, to Zachary if not to himself, that he could, figuratively, walk and chew gum at the same time when it came to simple household chores.

Well, the fire sure had blown that theory, hadn't it?

Not that Ryan had much time to think about that at the moment, because he was too busy glaring at the firemen as they ogled Janna in her towel.

"Can't you go back in through the front door and put some *clothes* on?" he growled from between clenched teeth when one of the firemen nearly tripped over the garden hose as he tried to enter the house and watch Janna at the same time. "I think you're about to cause a riot out here."

Janna looked down at the towel, looked at the firemen and then grimaced as a slow, rising flush turned her pink from chest to forehead. "Oops. I'll be right back. Try to find out how much damage you've—that is, how badly the house is damaged."

After speaking to the firemen, and to Zachary, Ryan felt he had learned some good news and some bad news. And some better than good news.

The bad news was that the ceiling of the kitchen had been damaged, so that the house needed some pretty hefty repair work...and that was over and above redoing the entire kitchen, and replacing the window and awning.

The good news was that the smoke damage was pretty much confined to the downstairs, and his personal check on the dining room mural showed it to be in pretty good shape.

The better news, to Ryan's mind, was that the smoke that had filtered up through the damaged ceiling and into the second floor had filtered straight into Janna's bedroom, which he felt could certainly only benefit from some redecorating anyway. And he wouldn't have to caulk. There was always that....

Not that he'd say as much to Janna.

The firemen had placed the last of the huge exhaust fans they'd brought, one in the kitchen, one in the front hallway, and were about ready to leave when Janna reappeared in the backyard.

She'd walked out the kitchen door, so Ryan knew she had now seen what he'd seen. Blistering blue paint on the walls. Smoke stains on everything. Charred curtains and cabinets; a ruined tile floor. A veritable flood of water damage everywhere.

A mess.

"You have some place to stay, ma'am?" one of the firemen asked her. "Because you're not going to be able to stay here for a while. That kitchen's a mess, and so is the ceiling. You know, another five minutes, and you probably would have lost the house. You've got quite a smart kid here. He did great with the hose."

"Yes, thank you," Janna said, running a hand through her still damp hair, her reddish curls looking, on the ends, like dark mahogany corkscrews. "Oh, and I have insurance, although I don't know if it covers putting us up in a hotel. I guess I'll have to call my agent."

"On a Saturday afternoon, ma'am? Good luck," the fireman said, shaking his head. "How did this fire get started anyway?"

It was, to Ryan's mind, a pity that Janna hadn't asked him to dig her a well today, because then he could have jumped into the hole and disappeared. Instead, as Zachary and Janna looked at him, he said, "It was all my fault, actually. I was too liberal with the firestarting stuff, whatever that's called."

The fireman nodded. "Happens more than you think. Well, you sure did make a mess, didn't you?"

Ryan smiled—oh, all right, he *grimaced,* rather evilly—at the fireman, wishing the guy and his jolly observations out of Janna's backyard.

"He's my handyman," Janna interjected, stepping closer to Ryan, almost as if she wanted to protect him, felt some need to protect him.

"Oh, yeah?" the fireman said, and now he looked at Ryan again, looked at him closely, appraisingly. "You insured, sir? Because you're probably going to have to pay for some of this, considering you were working here, and the fire was your fault. You did say it was your fault, right?''

"Don't you have a Stamp Out Forest Fires seminar to go to or something?'' Ryan asked the guy, who just shrugged, then finally followed after the other firemen, leaving Janna, Zachary and Ryan alone in the backyard.

Alone with the smell of smoke, the sight of a sadly melted metal frame of a denuded awning, and the sure knowledge that the day hadn't gone as planned.

"I'll pay for your hotel," Ryan offered. "And pay for anything your insurance doesn't cover."

"Uh-huh," Janna said, picking her way across the patio, past her ruined kitchen set that the firemen had dragged outside, and stepping into the kitchen.

Her bottom lip began to tremble. "Oh, look at the poor kitty!" she exclaimed, and at last she reacted. She began to cry. "The poor, poor kitty."

Ryan looked on the floor, expecting to see…well, he didn't want to think about what he might see. But Tansy was outside. He knew that because he'd seen Zachary holding the blue-cream cat. So he looked around some more, finally looking up, into the corner of the room, and saw the blue plastic clock.

Or what was left of it. It had been kitschy and silly. Now it looked like a Salvador Dali creation, the whole thing *melting* down the wall.

"We can find another one," he said weakly, wondering if such a thing was possible.

"No, we won't. She was one of the last of her breed," Janna said, sighing so that her shoulders rose and fell in her distress. "They just don't make them like that anymore."

"I can't imagine why not," Ryan said, then wanted

to kick himself as he heard his own words, heard the tone that was more mocking than concerned. Shame. Shame on him! One man's junk was another man's treasure, or so he'd heard. Obviously the cat was one of Janna Monroe's "treasures."

He tried to redeem himself. "The mural's still okay. I checked."

Janna turned to him, wiping away her tears and trying to smile. "Is it? That's good. Oh, I'm sorry. I'm being silly. After all, they're only *things.* You can always replace *things,* can't you? But I am glad about the mural. And there wasn't any damage in my office, although how I'm going to convince the insurance company that I'll need to have all my computers and stuff dragged to some hotel is beyond me."

"Office? Computers? I never asked. What do you do?"

Janna sniffed one last time, then led the way through the dining room and toward the stairs. He followed along as she told him about her business. "I design web pages for businesses who want to be on the Internet. Mark called it selling out, saying I should stay true to my fine arts training, but when Zachary was born, I went back to school, took the necessary computer classes, and started my own business."

"And you run that business out of this house? That would explain all the boxes of paper and stuff in the garage, wouldn't it? Yeah, right," Ryan said, following her down the hall to a closed door marked with a brass plaque that said "Unless you're bleeding or on fire, it isn't necessary to open this door."

"Cute sign," he said as Janna opened the door.

"It doesn't keep Zachary out, but at least he thinks twice now before he knocks," she told him, then stood just inside the door as Ryan looked around the room.

There were two desks, each with its own computer. A huge laser printer. Fax. Phones. Scanners. All the bits and pieces that make up the complete home office.

One of the computer screens was dark, but the other was lit by a screen saver that was nothing more than gold letters on a green background, the words swimming across the screen in a regular manner: No work, no pay.

"Succinct," Ryan said, pointing to the screen saver.

"I change it every week or so. Last week it said that butterflies are free, but hamburger costs real money." She pushed a hand through her tangled hair. "It helps keep me centered. Especially when I'd rather be outside, painting butterflies."

She put her hands on her hips, hips covered with another pair of jeans that fit her just a little too well for Ryan's comfort. She sighed yet again, her unfettered breasts rising and falling along with the form-fitting yellow T-shirt she wore.

She looked sixteen, going on thirty. She looked younger than spring, older than time. Simple as a Rubik's Cube, as easy to read as Sanskrit, and yet as strong as steel and as tough as nails.

Except for the hint of tears on her still-damp cheeks.

Except for the vulnerable posture of her shoulders.

Except for that too bright grin telling him that, no matter how brave a face she was putting on, she was about ready to collapse.

"Janna…I'm so sorry. There's got to be something

I can...some *way* I can...wait a minute! I have the perfect answer.''

''What's the question?'' Janna asked, picking up a glass paperweight and hefting its weight in her palm. She kept touching things, moving around the room and touching things, these things that all could be replaced, she had said. But her face told another story, and he knew she was thinking about all she could have lost.

All the memories she could have lost.

''My sister Maddy just got married a little while ago, and her apartment in the family house is empty. You'd each have your own bedroom with one still left over for this stuff. There's a living room and even a small dining room. A kitchen. It's on the third floor, and has its own entrance, if you don't want to go through the house.''

She looked at him as if he had just told her he was giving serious thought to going on the road as a stand-up comedian. ''You're kidding.''

Was he? He didn't think so. He meant it; he really meant it. She and Zachary could move into Maddy's old rooms until her house was repaired. Why not? Where would be the harm? What was the problem? What could go wrong?

Then he looked at Janna Monroe again. Looked at her closely. Thought about his grandmother, about Allie, who could take the slightest of threads and weave it into a whole cloth done up just to her design.

What could go wrong if he put Janna and Allie under the same roof?

Plenty!

And yet, he had no choice. The fire had been his fault. Janna's dilemma was all his fault. Hell, he'd burned her out of house and home, for crying out loud. You couldn't do much more damage than that without having to really, really work at it.

Besides, how long could it take to repair a kitchen, a ceiling? A week? Two? Three, at the most.

It wouldn't be so bad. And there was that separate entrance, so he and Janna Monroe didn't really even have to *see* each other.

"Please," Ryan said, touching Janna's arm as they headed back down the hall, and into her soot-darkened bedroom. "I'd feel so much better if you and Zachary came and stayed with us."

Janna walked to her closet and opened the double doors, pulling out a green-and-blue-flowered skirt, sniffing at it, wrinkling her nose at the smell of smoke that permeated the material.

"Does this apartment have its own washer and dryer?"

"It does," Ryan answered. He wasn't sure, not really, but if there were no washer and dryer now, there would be by tonight, if he had to buy an appliance store to get the job done.

"I could spend the next three days at some Laundromat, trying to get the stink out of all our clothes. Not that I have anything against Laundromats, but— all right," Janna said, holding out her hand to him, shaking his with some vigor. "In that case, we accept."

Chapter Four

"You burned down her *house?* You *burned down* her *house?* Oh, Ryan, that's *so* unlike you."

Ryan collapsed into an overstuffed chair, splaying his long legs out in front of him as he glared at his sister. "And what *would* be like me, Maddy?" he asked, feeling abused. More than merely abused. He felt like a fool, and he wasn't used to feeling like a fool.

"I don't know," Maddy answered, "not really. But burning down a woman's house just because she won you in the bachelor auction—well, it seems rather *excessive,* don't you think?"

Ryan looked at her owlishly. "I imagine I could have started with her garage. Except that I did such a damn good job of cleaning it that I don't think I could have brought myself to burning it down."

"You cleaned her garage?" Joe O'Malley asked, handing Ryan a bottled beer. "I wish you'd called first. I might have wanted to alert the local media."

Ryan grabbed the beer and took a long swallow. His sister and brother-in-law were enjoying themselves at his expense. And he couldn't blame them. He probably would have done the same.

"The fire aside—and, please, let's keep it there— I thought I should ask your permission for Ms. Monroe and her son to take over your apartment for a few weeks, Maddy."

She shrugged. "I don't live there anymore, Ryan, and the apartment *is* part of the family home. Of course I wouldn't mind. Although I guess I should go shovel out the rest of my stuff before Ms. Monroe arrives."

"Stuff? What stuff?" Joe asked. "This house is already crammed to the rafters with your stuff, my stuff, all our new stuff. We'll soon be known as the Stuffed O'Malleys. We could be served over rice."

"Let me know when you come to the punchline of that joke, darling. Oh, wait, I think you have, and it wasn't all that funny." Maddy rolled her eyes at her husband. "It's just turning into fall, Joe. Which, if you'd just think about it for a moment, might tell you that I haven't bothered to bring my winter wardrobe over here yet. I mean, we are only next door, so I couldn't see any reason to rush."

Joe winked at Ryan, then sat down dramatically, his eyes wide. "You have *more* clothes? Maddy, honey, Nieman-Marcus doesn't have *more* clothes."

Maddy stood up, smoothed down her denim skirt, and glared at the two men, both of whom were now chuckling into their beer bottles. "If we're all done here, I'll go next door and tell Allie what we're going to do."

Ryan hadn't had more than two sips of beer. He

wasn't at all drunk; not even a little tipsy. Still, he felt suddenly *sober*. He hopped to his feet, wincing as if Maddy's words had made a real physical impact on him. "Oh, God. Allie. I thought she was out playing golf. Isn't she playing golf?" He stabbed his fingers through his hair. "*Why* isn't she playing golf?"

Joe also got to his feet, slipping an arm around his wife's waist. "You know, it always amazes me how all three of you can be all grown-up, and still afraid of one small woman. Allie's a sweetheart, not the bogeyman."

Ryan and Maddy exchanged knowing glances. "He'll learn," they said together, then Ryan headed for the door, hoping he could head Janna Monroe off at the pass, before she rang the bell and met Allie.

He ran across the lawns separating his family home from that of his sister, and skidded to a halt at the front door, taking a moment to collect himself, to remind himself that he was a grown man, for crying out loud.

"He burned down your house?"

Janna walked around the drawing room, picking up small figurines that caught her eye, stopping to admire the very good art on the walls. "Mm-hmm," she answered vaguely, then added, "Is this a Picasso sketch? Good Lord, it is! I'd love to see all of your collection."

"Yes, yes, we'll take the grand tour later," Allie said distractedly, twisting about in her chair so that she could follow Janna's progress around the room. Honestly, the girl seemed as calm as if she'd just dropped in for a visit, and had not announced that her house had burned down and she was moving in for "the duration."

Janna was dressed in skintight jeans that, for some reason Allie would try to understand later, made her look wonderful but not at all tacky. Probably, she thought quickly, because the girl had the body of a top fashion model. Long, slim, perfectly proportioned.

And totally real, if that yellow sweater wasn't lying, and Allie doubted that it could.

Janna's mop of burnished curls was an amazement to Allie. Didn't the girl know what she had in that head of hair? How could she just *glomp* it all on top of her head with a rubber band and let it do what it wanted? Didn't she know that a good stylist would first weep, then set to work with scissors until the girl had a head of hair most women would kill to have?

But that wasn't the half of it. Not even a quarter of it. Allie had thought the girl to be *different,* just a bit out of the ordinary. Just the young woman to pull Ryan out of his self-imposed rut, shake him up a bit, get him to admit that there was more to life than balance sheets and three-piece suits and he really should be out there, living it.

But this girl? Could it be that she was *too* different?

Or could it be that Allie had suddenly sensed that there was no way in the world she could ever *control* Janna Monroe, not for a moment, no matter how right her plans might be, no matter how sane, how sensible.

Joe O'Malley hadn't been *controlled* by Allie, and she knew it. But Joe had wanted Maddy and Allie had shown him the way to get her. That had made him grateful, somewhat malleable. Allie liked her men malleable.

Matt Garvey, her granddaughter Jessica's husband,

had been much like Joe. Eager to please. Happy to listen. *Obedient*.

Neither were wimps, or whatever weak men were called these days. On the contrary, both men were successful businessmen, highly intelligent, and perfect mates for her two granddaughters.

Why, she'd even managed to get Joe's business partner, Larry, and Matt's sworn bachelorette sister, Linda, halfway to the altar. Indeed, she was expecting an announcement as soon as the lovestruck pair returned from their vacation in Jamaica. Allie took a certain amount of pride in the fact that *she* had played matchmaker for all three sets of lovers.

She hadn't really thought to play matchmaker by putting Janna Monroe in front of Ryan, or so she told herself again now. She'd just meant to shake him up, *wake* him up.

And it had been a good plan.

Until Ryan had burned down the woman's house!

Now here was Janna Monroe—Janna Monroe and her killer body, silly hair, unbelievably beautiful smile—and Allie, being a very intelligent women herself, suddenly realized that if there was a single person in the world able to resist her, it was this same Janna Monroe.

Not that Allie didn't admire a woman of independence, a woman with a mind truly her own. It was just that Janna Monroe seemed a little *too* independent. A little too easygoing. A little too—dare she think it, say it?—*flaky*.

Perhaps it was time to remind Janna Monroe of a few facts.

"I regret how this has all worked out, my dear," Allie said kindly. "When I had you bid on my grandson for me, I had no idea it would cost you your house.''

Janna, her cursory inventory of the room complete, sat down in a chair across from Allie, her long legs twisted in the Lotus position as she grinned at the woman. "Not the whole house, Mrs. Chandler. Just the kitchen. And a little bit of my bedroom and bath. And he did put the fire out, so it wasn't as if he had done it on purpose. Did I tell you that Zachary is in your backyard? I think I did. Zachary's my son. He's nine and three-quarters and completely housebroken. I hope you don't mind that he wanted to look around. I think he's hoping to find a swing set or a jungle gym."

The woman had a *son?*

This was what happened with off-the-cuff, spur-of-the-moment plans. They always had flaws. Ryan would never be interested in a woman with a child. In fact, now that she really thought about it, all her two thousand dollars had bought her was a pair of live-in problems…and Ryan probably even more entrenched in his dull life than ever before.

But, back to the child, Allie told herself. In life, as in golf or tennis, it was never a good thing not to keep your eye on the ball.

"Your son will find a gazebo and a pool and a tennis court," Allie answered with a wave of her hand. "I hope he doesn't feel underprivileged by our lack of amenities. The pool has a diving board," she added as Janna continued to look at her, *stare* at her, those wide brown eyes seemingly able to see straight through her.

"This isn't what you wanted, is it?" Janna asked after a moment. "I mean, I know what you said the night of the auction. That Ryan was in a rut, bored, needed some excitement in his life. I told you I was looking for a tall man, a handyman, to get some chores done around the house. And you loved it, didn't you? You thought a day with me, getting his hands dirty, might just wake poor Ryan up, shake him back to life—and all that other stuff you said. But you didn't plan on having Zach and me move in here for a few weeks, did you?''

Allie bent her head, pretended to inspect the pocket on her skirt. She'd been right. The girl could see straight through her. ''I didn't think he'd burn down your house, certainly. Ryan has always seemed much more…competent.''

Janna laughed out loud. ''He probably is, in his own world. I stuck him into mine, and I can tell you, it wasn't a comfortable fit. So don't worry, Mrs. Chandler, I'm not out to seduce the guy or anything.''

Ryan's timing had been impeccable for most of his life. But his timing, his grandmother thought now, couldn't have been worse today, as she looked up at the sound of a rather strangled *"What?"* to see him standing just at the entrance to the drawing room.

Immediately, Allie rallied. She hadn't, after all, been exactly down, and she certainly hadn't been out. Not Almira Chandler. Not by a long shot! She had been just about to charm Janna Monroe into doing whatever she asked—truly, she was—and she'd be darned if she'd let Ryan's inopportune entrance make things worse than they already were.

And they were already pretty bad. Even the usually optimistic Allie knew that.

''Darling!'' she exclaimed, hopping up from her chair to glide over to Ryan, motion for him to bend down so that he could kiss her cheek. "Have you come here after signing up for therapy about this newly discovered pyromania of yours? And to think, as a child you never once tried to play with matches."

"Matches were too tame. I was waiting for you to buy some acetylene torches," Ryan said, looking at Janna, who was now standing, her hands behind her back, rocking on her heels. "I see you two have already met."

Janna's grin twisted something somewhere deep in his gut. He'd never met a woman so determinedly cheerful in the face of what another woman—a *sane* woman—would have seen as a total disaster. "Heard us, did you?" she asked. "How much did you hear? Were your ears wagging out there in the hallway for long?"

With another woman, any other woman, Ryan would have politely lied. He might even have defended his own eavesdropping, if he really didn't like the woman.

But Janna wasn't like any other woman, and he did like her. He'd didn't know *why,* but he liked her.

"I heard you promise not to seduce me," he told her as he escorted Allie back over to the conversation grouping in the center of the large room. "I don't know about anyone else, but I'll sleep easier tonight," he ended, feeling his mouth widen into a grin he hadn't expected.

He watched as Janna and Allie exchanged quick looks, and thought he caught his grandmother shaking her head in the negative. "What? What did I miss?"

"Well, you might have missed overhearing that it was your grandmother who paid for my bid the other night," Janna said innocently…as Allie groaned and sank as far into the sofa cushions as she could manage. "Or did you really think I'd pay two thousand dollars for a handyman?"

Allie groaned again. It was even worse than she thought. The dratted woman was *honest*. How on earth could she deal with an open, honest woman, a woman with no guile? She had to get this girl gone, then go back to the drawing board, find a suitable young woman for her grandson. How fast could carpenters and sundry other repairmen work?

Ryan sat very still, looking at Janna. Looking at his grandmother. He didn't say a word.

He didn't have to. All he had to do was wait.

"Now, Ryan. Darling," Allie said at last, filling the silence Ryan had provided for her. "Don't be angry. I had to make sure you got the highest bid, didn't I? After all, we're Chandlers. We have a certain *standard* to maintain. What if someone bid more for someone like Charlie? Wouldn't you have been devastated?"

"*You* bid on Charlie, and ran the bidding up twice as far as it should have gone," Ryan reminded his grandmother.

"Yes, but I felt sorry for him, among other things. And don't change the subject. Besides, I could have offered my checkbook to Marcia. Be happy I chose Janna here. Be grateful."

Ryan stood up, began to pace. "Oh, that's beautiful, Allie. Just beautiful. First you meddle in my life, and then you want me to be *grateful* that you didn't meddle *more*."

Janna wrinkled up her nose—she looked so *cute*, wrinkling up her nose—and headed for the doorway with her long, fluid strides. "I think I'll leave you two alone to sort this out. I'll be out back, with Zachary, who probably thinks he's died and gone to hog heaven.''

Allie fought the urge to call Janna back, knowing that the girl wasn't exactly an ally. Maybe a buffer of sorts? And she did like the girl. Perhaps she liked her too much, because Ryan certainly couldn't. He was her grandson, and she loved him, but he was much too much the stuffed shirt ever to fall for a free spirit like Janna Monroe.

Oh well, she'd just have to muddle through the best she could.

"Now, Ryan," she began reasonably. "I don't see any need to be upset. I was *not* matchmaking. I mean, any fool can see that you and that long, tall Pollyanna wouldn't suit. You don't have a single thing in common, most especially your taste in clothing.''

"She's a very nice woman," Ryan interjected, rather angrily, which surprised him.

"Nice? Oh. Oh, of course she is, darling," Allie responded, the wheels in her mind doing double time in their always rapid rotations. "But nice? Is that enough? She certainly isn't compatible with your lifestyle, now is she?''

"My lifestyle," Ryan repeated. "What in hell is my lifestyle, Allie? Can you describe it to me?''

Allie began doing mental handsprings, but her long practice in hiding her motives came to her rescue just in time. "Oh, I don't know, darling. Dull, straitlaced. *Boring?* Certainly not as *colorful* as Ms. Monroe's lifestyle. She's an artist, isn't she? No, no. How could you possibly think I was trying to maneuver you into an association with Janna Monroe? You'd bore her to death and she'd drive you crazy. I'm good, darling, but not even I could believe yours would be a match made in heaven.''

''Is that so?'' Ryan said, his head bobbing up and down like a cork on a choppy sea. ''Is that so? Well, that just goes to show what you know, Allie. I think Janna's wonderful.''

''You do?'' Allie frowned on the outside. Inside, she was rapidly amending plans and doing a jig.

''Yes. Yes, I do. She's a widow raising a son alone—and Zach's a good kid, as far as kids go. She's got her own business, a house—well, she used to have a house. She's pretty, in her own way. What's not to like?''

Allie produced a long-suffering sigh that, if nominated, would have easily won the Oscar for Best Performance by a Busybody. ''Well, if you *insist*, darling, I suppose I won't stand in your way....''

''Damn straight you won't!'' Ryan declared, then suddenly shut his mouth, slapped a hand against his forehead. ''What am I *saying?*''

Allie stood on tiptoe, reached up and patted her grandson's cheek. ''Well, darling, if you don't know, I'm certainly not going to tell you. And now I'm off to see Mrs. Ballantine and tell her there will be two extra for dinner. Oh, and I hope you don't mind if we decide against the barbecued steaks we'd been considering. Ta-ta!''

Ryan watched his grandmother go, his eyes narrowed as he mentally reviewed their conversation, wondering when Allie's try at reverse psychology had begun to work so well...too well.

Then he shrugged his shoulders and said aloud, ''Does it matter?'' and went off to find Janna and her son.

He found them in the backyard, inspecting the pool.

"Hi," Janna said, waving to him as he walked across the lawn. "Zachary was just trying to convince me that nobody would mind if he stripped to his underwear and took a dip. The thermometer over by the pool house is registering almost seventy-five degrees in the sun. What do you think?"

Ryan thought that Mrs. Ballantine, should that good woman look out the kitchen window, would have a conniption not seen since the day Maddy had been learning how to cook and turned on the blender without first tapping on the lid. It had been amazing, just how far a few mashed bananas could fly in a room the size of the Chandler kitchen.

"The pool is heated, so I don't see why not, although he's going to freeze when he comes out," he said, and Zachary emitted a happy shout, then quickly stripped out of his shorts and sneakers before diving in at the deep end. "Unless he can't swim," he added, watching, waiting for Zachary to surface once more.

"Zach? He's a *fish*," Janna said proudly. "So, are we still welcome? I mean, that was a pretty nasty trick, wasn't it? Having your grandmother advance me the bid money. Although I felt a little better upping the amount to two thousand, because she thought she could get you for fifteen hundred. And it was all for a good cause, right? You swim?"

Ryan sorted through Janna's words, then looked at Zachary, who had climbed out of the pool at the other end and was now dancing on the tiles, shivering and hugging himself. "Not in September I don't, even if this is the warmest day we've had in a while. You think we should get him a towel?"

"I don't think you should build him a fire," Janna

countered, then laughed. "Oh, I'm sorry," she said
quickly, touching his arm. "That was low."

"I'll live," Ryan responded as the two of them
headed for the small pool house that had changing
rooms and a supply of towels. "I'm just sorry I can't
say the same for your cat. The one on the wall, that
is."

He grabbed up two towels and handed them to
Janna, who was soon wrapping a shivering Zachary
in one while she dried his dripping hair with the other.
"I really loved that clock," she admitted on a sigh.
"It was just so…so…*ugly*. Oh, and speaking about
cats—is anyone in your house allergic? Because I refuse to put Tansy in a kennel until the house is repaired. After all, the fire wasn't her fault."

"Bringing us, yet again, full circle to whose fault
it was," Ryan said, leading the way to the outside
entrance to the apartment that took up half of the third
floor. His own apartment, not quite as large, took up
the other half, not that he was about to mention that
right now.

"It was my fault, too, Mom," Zachary said
bravely. "I forgot to tell him to move the kettle out
from under the awning. Are you mad at me?"

Janna went straight down on her knees in front of
her son, cupping his chin in her hand as she spoke to
him. "I am *not* angry with you, Zachary. You were
splendid, holding the hose as Mr. Chandler asked, not
trying to get back into the house to rescue any of your
things. The fire was an accident, nothing more." She
looked up at Ryan. "Nobody's to blame."

"'You're a better man than I am, Gunga Din,'"
Ryan grumbled, knowing he probably wouldn't be so

forgiving of anyone who had, damn it, burned down *his* house.

"Kipling. One of my favorites." Janna smiled and let Zachary pull her to her feet. "Besides, we're going to have a great adventure, aren't we, Zach? Now, let's go see our new home. Meet me upstairs after you get Tansy's pet carrier from the car, okay? Then we'll go back to the house and pick up another load of stuff. You'll help, won't you, Ryan? Just with the computers."

"Do I have a choice?"

Janna considered this for a moment, then said, "Nope. I don't think you do."

"I didn't think so." Ryan watched as Zachary obediently ran to the garage area, then transferred his attention to Janna as she—and her marvelous jeans—led the way up the stairs to the apartment, wondering just how much of this "great adventure" he might be lucky enough to survive.

Chapter Five

Janna had thought he'd never leave.

One way or the other, she'd been in Ryan Chandler's company since early that morning. Now, at five o'clock, she was finally on her own, pretty much surrounded by her own belongings, if not her own house, and she wanted, *needed,* some time to think.

Her house had nearly burned down.

There was a thought to occupy her mind for a while.

A thought that could occupy her for much longer, much, much longer, was how little she was concerned over her ruined kitchen and how badly she felt that Ryan Chandler felt bad.

Poor guy. She'd watched his face all afternoon. Saw the embarrassment. The self-directed disgust. The feelings of helplessness. The anger mixed with frustration directed at that sweet, conniving old lady, Almira Chandler.

And now—now that Janna and Zachary were living

in his house—Ryan's badly hidden anxiety that, if nothing much could be worse than burning down a woman's house, there had to be something about to happen thanks to this awkward arrangement that probably would be.

She'd recognized the same look on Almira Chandler's face, actually, although that look hadn't lasted. The older woman's shock at seeing Janna in her drawing room had been quickly covered with a gracious welcome and a genteel smile. But with the announcement, "We're moving in," Almira's smile appeared to be painted in place, not growing naturally at all.

Janna had had just enough time to herself—as Zachary had chosen to ride with Ryan on their several trips between the two houses—to figure out that Almira Chandler had carefully picked her out of all the women in that crowded ballroom because she had *stood out* from all the other women in that crowded ballroom.

Stuck out like a sore thumb, actually.

And then the woman had all but sicced her on her grandson, hoping to shake him up, wake him up. Sort of like a little comic relief from the village idiot, meant to get him up off his duff and out into the world a little. Just enough, of course, to show him there was a whole world outside his own small society…and not enough to have him actually thinking about inviting that small "diversion" home to supper.

Well, Almira Chandler might not have counted on her, but she'd gotten her anyway, and she'd have her until the house was repaired.

Which, Janna decided as she sank into the huge, claw-footed bathtub in the large, old-fashioned bathroom, wasn't all that much of a hardship. Not when you got right down to it.

Zachary was having fun. Tansy seemed to like the wide windowsills. Her computers had all fit neatly into the spare bedroom. A second load of clothes was already sloshing around in the washer in the laundry room off the galley kitchen.

Antique furniture. Persian rugs. Fresh flowers on the tables. Real art on the walls. Down pillows—she'd checked—on the beds.

All the place needed was a blue cat clock.

"May I come in?"

Janna, who had been lying back in the tub, her neck supported on the rim by a fluffy towel, opened her eyes…and saw a red-lipped crow standing beside her.

Well, not actually a crow. But the woman was dressed all in black, had a tight black bun on the top of her head, and the red slash of lipstick sure did make its own statement. What it *said,* Janna wasn't sure, but it sure did tell her this was a woman with some hidden fires she couldn't quite keep tamped down.

Picking up a handful of bubbles and blowing on it, just to see the bubbles scatter, Janna smiled up at the woman. "I have a choice?" she asked as the woman pulled a small white-and-gold vanity chair from beneath the dressing table and sat down.

"I'm Mrs. Ballantine," the woman said, and Janna watched, fascinated, as the red slash of mouth tried to smile. "I'm the housekeeper here, and have been for more years than you've had hot dinners, as the saying goes. I thought I ought to let you know what's happening here."

"What's happening here?" Janna repeated, wincing. Now she was playing parrot to the crow. "I think I'm taking a bath."

Mrs. Ballantine stood up, plucked a towel from the heated rack. "You *were* taking a bath. Dinner is in fifteen minutes. We dine promptly around here. I insist on it."

"I'll just bet you do," Janna said, then decided it might be easier to go with the flow. Besides, the woman intrigued her. How could someone as bright and sunny as Almira Chandler get along with someone so dark and dramatic as Mrs. Ballantine?

The answer, of course, was that there was more to Almira Chandler than met the eye, that she wanted someone like Janna to see. Nothing mysterious, though, she was sure of that. She hadn't been suddenly catapulted into some gothic novel, or wandered back to *Rebecca's* Manderly—the kitchen fire notwithstanding, of course.

With her usual lack of embarrassment, Janna stood up in the tub, stepped out, and allowed Mrs. Ballantine to drape her with the huge bath sheet. "Thank you," she said, grabbing a second towel for her hair, as she had showered out the worst of the smut and smoke before filling the tub. "Now, let me guess. I'm just taking a wild stab at it, but I think I've got it right. You're Mrs. Chandler's cohort in crime. Ying to her Yang, and all that good stuff. Right?"

"We had a mutual fondness for Mr. Chandler," Mrs. Ballantine said stiffly, then a look of horror passed over her raisin eyes. "Oh, nothing like *that*," she corrected herself quickly. "But someone has to take care of the woman, or else she'd go flying straight off the ground with her silliness."

"Of course," Janna agreed, walking over to the

sink and pulling off the towel that hid her riot of curls. "Gonna scare the kiddies tonight, if I'm not careful," she said, pushing at her tangled curls. "I think I forgot my blow dryer. Is there one around here, do you think?"

In answer, the housekeeper went to a wall lined with white-painted closets and opened a set of double doors with a flourish. Inside was a veritable treasure trove of toiletries, heated curler appliances, curling irons...and three different blow dryers. "Miss Maddy liked to try new things," she said in way of explanation. "She's already phoned to tell me that you're to feel free to use anything you need. She's like that, very generous. They're all generous. To a fault, sometimes."

"Miss Maddy? That would be Maddy O'Malley? Wife of the software king, Joe O'Malley?"

When Mrs. Ballantine looked at her, looked down her nose at her, Janna grinned and added, "Mr. Chandler spoke of her earlier today. And of Jessica Garvey, his other sister. The one expecting the twins. Twins are nice, don't you think? Although Zachary *seemed* like twins when he was in the terrible twos. Is there anything else, Mrs. Ballantine?"

"Just a warning," the housekeeper said, once more making herself comfortable on the small chair.

"A warning," Janna repeated, dropping the towel onto the floor and picking up the underclothing she'd brought into the bathroom with her. "That sounds ominous."

"It isn't," Mrs. Ballantine said, and Janna thought, just for an instant, that the woman had actually smiled. "It's just that Almira Chandler doesn't get her comeuppance very often, so you'd better be on your guard for a while, until she figures out that she planned all of this—even if she didn't. She needs to feel in charge, you understand.''

''She's going to figure out some way to take blame for the fire?'' Janna shook her head. ''I don't think so.''

''Not the fire, miss,'' Mrs. Ballantine said as she picked up the two discarded towels and stuffed them in a large wicker hamper that had to date back to the 1930s. ''Allow me to explain.''

''Gladly,'' Janna, now clad in an almost nonexistent pink bra and French cut cotton panties, said as she stood at the mirror and tried, without much success, to pull a comb through her wet curls.

''Mrs. Chandler submitted Mr. Chandler's name to the bachelor auction in order to get him out of the office, away from his work and back into life a little. She assumed, quite incorrectly—although anyone with any sense would never point that out to her— that he'd get a *kick* out of the silliness of the thing, and maybe even want to start dating again. Mr. Ryan hasn't had a date in six months, miss. We were beginning to worry.''

''Six months, huh?'' Janna mentally calculated the date of her own last trip into the social world, and winced. ''Man, if you were worried about him, you'd have to be terrified for me. I haven't been out on a date in two years.''

Mrs. Ballantine snorted. Really. A snort. ''That's nothing. Try thirty years, and see what a cakewalk *that* is,'' she said, then straightened her shoulders and continued. ''Mrs. Chandler was in the audience that night, as you know. What you don't know is that she saw you talking to Mr. Ryan, then saw Mr. Ryan watching you rather, um, *closely* as you walked away. Until that moment, she had actually believed she was allowing nature to take its course, which, of course, is not at all in Mrs. Chandler's nature. Are you following me, miss?''

''Hanging on your every word, Mrs. B,'' Janna said brightly, pulling an orange-and-green-flowered cotton dress over her head, allowing the soft material to fall straight to her ankles.

''To hear Mrs. Chandler tell it, she had a flash of brilliance at that moment, believing that, of all the women in the ballroom that night, *you'd* be the perfect one to pull Mr. Ryan out of his doldrums. Were you really wearing combat boots, miss, or did Mrs. Chandler make that part up?''

''I always knew those boots would get me into trouble one day. Darn,'' Janna said, trying not to giggle.

''Please be serious, miss. Remember, I've come here to warn you.''

''Warn me about what? I already know most of what you've said, and guessed the rest. I was to be the carrot to the donkey, or whatever. I was *not*, however, supposed to be more than a single day's diversion. Of course, that was before Ryan, obviously never an Eagle Scout no matter how fine his other virtues, burned down my kitchen. So what's next? Am I to remember that I was only supposed to be around for one day? Am I supposed to be a very good girl, keep to my rooms and not try to corrupt good old, boring Ryan? I mean, fun's fun and all that, but nobody was looking to have me around for weeks and weeks, right?''

''Wrong,'' Mrs. Ballantine said, standing very

straight as she smoothed the front of her black dress. "Oh, it may not have started out that way, and Mrs. Chandler was unexpectedly slow to realize her own brilliance—her words, definitely not mine, miss. But now? Now that you're here? You and your son? Well, Mrs. Chandler now believes that she must have subconsciously *known* all along that she'd found the perfect mate for her only grandson."

Janna dropped the comb in the sink and turned to look at the housekeeper. "You're kidding, right?"

"You've been warned, Miss Monroe," Mrs. Ballantine answered, "and forewarned is forearmed."

"Really? And a stitch in time saves nine?"

The housekeeper frowned. "I don't believe you're considering the seriousness of this situation."

"Oh, I am, I am," Janna said. "Except that I can't see one teensy-weensy part of all of this—that being why *you* should be so concerned. It isn't exactly as if I'm facing some fate worse than death, now is it?"

"What happens to you is no concern of mine, Miss Monroe," Mrs. Ballantine informed her most sincerely. "It's just that I see a lot of Mrs. Chandler in you and, now that you know her plans, now that you understand the whole of it...well, I thought it might be fun to sit back and watch the show. I haven't had a good laugh in a long time."

"Yeah," Janna grumbled under her breath. "I could tell. Well," she said, rallying, "I want to thank you for your warning. I'm still not sure what it *is,* but thank you anyway. I'll be on the lookout, making sure I'm not maneuvered into anything I don't want, okay?"

"Just remember to stand your ground and give as good as you get," Mrs. Ballantine concluded, and swept out of the bathroom, calling back over her shoulder, "Eight minutes, Miss Monroe. Please be prompt—and make sure the child washes his grubby little hands before coming to the table."

Janna had been an only child, as had Mark. Zachary was their only child. She'd always known she'd been missing something in not having a large family, and she found out exactly what she had been missing during that first Saturday night family dinner at the Chandler table.

Laughter. This family laughed a lot, sometimes at each other's expense, and sometimes just for the fun of it.

Jessica Chandler Garvey, the mother-to-be, was spending a lot of time poking fun at herself tonight, saying that "this eating for three is killing me," even as she snatched a freshly buttered roll from her husband's hand before it could quite reach his mouth. "But what a way to go," she'd ended, licking butter from her fingertips.

Maddy, who had prepared the main course of rump roast and oven-roasted potatoes, stabbed at a roasted carrot and waved it under her sister's nose. "Vitamins, Jessica. Vitamins and minerals and beta-whatever. And besides, they taste good. Try them."

Matt Garvey shook his head. "We all know how much Jessica hates vegetables. It's enough that we can get four glasses of milk down her every day, right, Jess?"

"If Maddy really loved me," Jessica responded, "she'd find a way to make chocolate-covered broccoli."

Zachary watched everyone with his brown eyes almost dancing in his head; all these young, vibrant, beautiful people, and all of them so happy, so carefree, so obviously fond of each other.

"You guys are *cool*," he said at last, so that Janna had to bite her bottom lip to keep from laughing out loud. "Do you do this every night, or is this just some special occasion—you know, like Christmas? Mom and me eat in the dining room sometimes, but mostly we just sit at the kitchen table or put up trays in front of the TV. But this is like a restaurant," he said as Mrs. Ballantine placed another tray of rolls on the table. "With waitresses and everything!"

Now Janna did laugh out loud, because the look on Mrs. Ballantine's face was priceless, simply priceless.

"I am *not* a waitress, young man, I am the housekeeper. And take your elbows off the table. Were you raised in a barn?"

"No, ma'am," Zachary said, quickly hiding his hands in his lap. "Sorry, ma'am."

"That's it, Mrs. B., whip the boy into shape, just the way you did us," Ryan said from the head of the table. "And then you can take him into the kitchen and wash his face. Can anyone else remember Mrs. B. grabbing us by the back of the head while she *mashed* a washcloth into our faces?"

"Please," Maddy said, picking up her wineglass. "No horror stories in front of the child. But we love you, Mrs. Ballantine," she added, tipping back her head to look up at the housekeeper. "Truly we do."

"Harrumph!" the housekeeper said, then sailed out of the room, barely able to keep her smile hidden from everyone—everyone but Janna, that was, because she had been watching closely.

"You've got a lovely home, Mrs. Chandler,"

Janna said during a small lull in the almost constant conversation.

"I imagine you did, too, my dear," Allie answered from the foot of the table, "until my grandson burned it down, that is."

"Allie…" Ryan began in a near growl, so that Matt quickly broke in, telling Janna about the day he and Jessica had left pancakes and bacon cooking on the stove, forgetting about them until the smoke alarm went off.

"It's the smirks of the firemen that are the worst of it," Jessica stated, stabbing at a carrot and reluctantly popping it into her mouth. "They want to know all the gory details, almost as if they're putting together a scrapbook of the World's Stupidest Fires. It was *so* embarrassing."

"I'll bet the local firemen are already writing the chapter on your fire, Ryan," Joe said with a wink. "Tell me again—how did the fire start? Something about you actually *trying* to start it?"

"Ryan," Janna interrupted quickly, grabbing at the first conversational gambit she could think of to save him further embarrassment, "did you know there's a Civil War reenactment going on this weekend? Both the Union and Confederate armies, real camps where the soldiers sleep overnight, and then battles during the day. Zachary and I are planning to go there tomorrow. Would you like to come along?"

"Saved by the pretty lady in the flowered dress," Joe whispered to Maddy, who rapped him on the wrist with her spoon.

Ryan looked down the table at Janna, surprisingly not so much in gratitude than in real interest. "I've seen the signs, but I hadn't actually thought about attending. Yes, yes, I will go. It sounds like fun.''

"Great!" Janna said, grinning at Almira Chandler. If there was going to be a battle, she might as well take the first shot. "Maybe your grandmother would like to come along. Although it is on a rather hilly site. Do you think she's up to it?"

"Sit back," Maddy warned her husband. "There's going to be crockery flying down the table in a moment.''

"Up to it?" Allie repeated, pressing one splayed hand against her breast. "Did you actually ask if I'm *up* to it? Oh, my dear child…" she purred, which was never a good sign—and you could ask any Chandler child and get that same answer.

And then, much to everyone's surprise, Allie lifted her shoulders, let them drop. "Oh, you're so right, my dear. The spirit so willing, the flesh so weak. But I thank you, truly I do, for the invitation. Just you and Ryan and the boy go. Have fun. Perhaps you could bring me a souvenir?"

Janna watched Ryan watch his grandmother, then she caught Mrs. Ballantine wink at her as the housekeeper refilled Zachary's milk glass. "I'm sure we could rent a wheelchair for you, Mrs. Chandler," Mrs. Ballantine said. "Or maybe one of those motorized carts?"

"Isn't there something in the kitchen that needs *stuffing*, Mrs. Ballantine?" Allie drawled, then smiled at Janna once more. "Shall we have our dessert in the drawing room?"

"Let me help you up," Ryan said as he nearly raced to the bottom of the table to pull out Allie's chair. "Mustn't overdo, you know."

"Do you want me to go with you, darling?" Allie whispered so that only Ryan could hear as she leaned on his arm, heading toward the drawing room. "Keep this up, and I'll be there with bells on. Which might not be a bad idea, as you probably need all the help you can get."

"Help doing what, Allie?" Ryan asked. "I think I know how to get myself entangled, or unentangled, without your help."

"You've needed it so far," she reminded him, then dropped her hand from his arm and sat herself down on the couch. "All of you have."

Janna sat down beside Almira just in time to see the quizzical look on Ryan's face, because they had both heard the slight tremor in Allie's voice.

And Janna instantly knew why she'd heard it. Almira Chandler was a wonderful woman, a dear woman. But she lived for her family, and needed her family to live for her. That was rather sad.

She patted Allie's hand. "You must be so proud of your grandchildren, Mrs. Chandler," she said brightly. "It's a night like this that shows me how much Zachary and I have missed in not having a family of our own close by. There's nothing like the love and wisdom of an older generation to anchor a family, is there?"

"Ha," Allie said, rallying back to her usual self. "An anchor around my *neck* is more like it, my dear. Why, if you only knew the *trouble* I've had riding herd on this helpless, hopeless group...."

Janna smiled, and listened, and felt Ryan's eyes on her for the next hour, then took Zachary up to bed, for it had been a long day.

What a strange and wonderful family, she thought

snuggling on a flowered chintz couch loaded with a dozen comfy cushions after Zachary was tucked in. Strange and wonderful and quite remarkable. The true matriarchal family. Almira Chandler, Janna decided, was just the sort of woman she wanted to be when she grew up: smart, sassy and probably dangerous.

It was a good thing Mrs. Ballantine had delivered her warning. Otherwise, Janna was pretty sure Almira Chandler would have Ryan and herself married and honeymooning before they knew what was happening to them....

Chapter Six

As if on orders from one of the two "armies," the September weather was cooperating wonderfully; the air warm and sweet, the temperature mild, the sun bright.

By ten o'clock the "campgrounds," actually part of the local park system, were bustling with life as reenactors and visitors tramped up and down the hillside of long grass and winding paths.

Ryan had parked his car in one of the designated lots, then made a contribution to a small boy wearing the uniform of a Union drummer boy, who handed him a thin program.

"Did we miss anything, huh, did we miss anything?" Zachary asked, trying to jump up and down beside Ryan, obviously believing he'd be able to read bits of the program on the up part of each jump. "Mom's such a *nag,* making us go to church every Sunday. I'll bet we missed something."

"Nope," Ryan assured him, reading through the

program before tucking it in his back pocket. They were walking uphill now, past a few stands selling refreshments and souvenirs. "So far, all they've done is make their own breakfast over open fires, and clean up their tents. Right now the reenactors are giving talks about the war and how it was fought, how the soldiers lived. They don't start shooting at each other for another hour or so."

"Cool. That's the best part, you know. We were here last year, and the year before that. The Yankees get the top of the hill, and the Rebels are down at the bottom—you'll see, once we get to the top of the hill. The Rebels are in the trees down at the bottom on the other side, and they attack by running straight uphill, into the Yankee guns. It's *awesome!*"

"I'm hoping to work in the finer points of the whys and hows, the history and lessons to be learned, of course," Janna said as Zachary ran ahead, straight in the direction of the wooden tower that sat on the crest of the hill. "But, for now, Zachary's mostly interested in the shooting."

Ryan smiled and took Janna's hand, as the path was steep and taking her hand was the gentlemanly thing to do. It was also nice. Nice to be seen with this happy, carefree, totally outrageous woman dressed in an ankle-length, striped, wraparound skirt that could have been made directly from Joseph's coat of many colors, topped by another of those clingy sweaters— and a mop of hair for the moment concealed beneath a straw sun hat as large as some dining room tables.

And the boots. He couldn't forget the boots. The boots, the makeup-free, shiny nose, the wide, unaffected smile…the complete assurance with which she carried herself, as if she were happy with herself and couldn't care less what the rest of the world might think.

"I've got to know," Ryan said at last. "Where in *hell* did you ever find that hat?"

"You like it?" Janna asked, pulling it off, plucking at the mound of silk flowers that danced around the brim. "It was the booby prize at Zachary's Parents' Night fund-raiser auction. Although why anyone would think anything this wonderful could be a booby prize, I'll never know."

"Just imagine," Ryan said, seeing that Janna was serious. She really *liked* the hat. And so did he, he realized with some shock. On anyone else it would be silly, out of place. But on Janna? Janna of the wild colors and long, booted strides and vibrant love of life? On her it looked good.

"Oh, look, they're all done, darn it," Janna said, pulling on his hand as she began to trot toward the wooden tower. "Now you won't hear the explanation about the towers, and it's *so neat!*"

Ryan stood beside the tower, looking up at the place where a soldier would stand, exposed, to watch for sign of the enemy. "I think I know about these," he told Janna, who had sat down in the long grass, pulling a chocolate bar out of some hidden pocket in her skirt. "There weren't any walkie-talkies or anything during the Civil War, so when messages had to be sent to outlying troops, these towers were the means of communication."

"Right," Janna said, breaking off half of the chocolate bar and handing it to him. "And the soldiers in the towers cupped their hands around their mouths, and yelled to each other."

Ryan dropped his head, shook it. "I know you're

teasing me, but *no,* that's not how it was done. They used these flags," he said, pulling one of the large flags free from its bracket on one of the support posts. "They used different colored flags, and movement codes, to warn of advancing attack, to redirect the troops in the field, and to pass messages across the miles. But you knew that, right?"

"Right," Janna said, picking a leggy blue wild-flower and tucking it into the band of her hat. "It was the most dangerous mission of any in either army, as the first thing the enemy would do was to try to destroy the towers." She stood up, looked at him quizzically. "Not many people know about the towers."

Ryan used his index finger to push his sunglasses up on the bridge of his nose. "I like history, especially American history. It's…it's a hobby of mine."

"Really? And yet you've never been to this reenactment before? I think that sign back there said this is their fourteenth year at this same site."

I've been busy seemed too lame an excuse, so Ryan just smiled and pointed to the triple row of small, white tents that were the camp of the Union Army. "Either men were shorter in the 1860s, or the soldiers all slept with their feet outside the tents," he said, taking her hand and walking toward the small knot of people listening to one of the reenactors talking about the equipment each foot soldier carried with him in the field, while Zachary wandered off to do a little exploring of his own.

"In the field," the reenactor was saying, "the soldier's gear included everything he needed, if not all the comforts of home. Inside this small kit, for instance— Hey, Janna!" he said, breaking off from his prepared talk. "Which side are you going to be rooting for this year?"

"Hiya, George," Janna said, waving to him as Ryan stood beside her, realizing he wasn't quite as shocked as he might have been, even should have been. It almost seemed *natural* for the man to know Janna, for everyone to know Janna. And like her. "I haven't made up my mind yet. But I was thinking of working on my Southern drawl, so maybe you'll be looking down the business end of my bayonet soon, huh?"

"In your dreams, Monroe," the Union "soldier" said, hiking up his belt around his rather ample belly. "But if we can't have you, we'll take Zach. Beats a good drum, that kid."

"You've got a deal," Janna said, waving at him before moving away, allowing George to resume his talk. "George is my garbage man," she explained as she and Ryan headed toward the line of small cannon farther down the hillside. "Although he likes to call himself a garbologist. He's always bringing me treasures he finds in the garbage, because of my parents, you understand."

"No, not really," Ryan said, his mind beginning to buzz in the comfortable heat of a bright sun. "What do your parents have to do with garbage?"

"A lot, actually," Janna answered, then quickly covered her ears, for the "army" was testing one of the cannon. After the boom died away, she continued, "My parents—they're somewhere in Asia right now, I think—are archeologists. They've been digging through other people's garbage for a long time. It just sounds fancier when you call it all artifacts."

"Archeologists? Really? And I thought you said you had no family. You did say that, didn't you?"

Janna skipped a little ahead of Ryan, heading downhill toward the Confederate camp, still hidden by the trees. "Poor Sam and Mary, not gone, but still forgotten," she teased, dancing in place as three mounted soldiers trotted by, saluting her as they passed. "No, no, they're very much alive. They're just not *around* much, you understand? I used to travel with them, when I was a kid, which was a lot of fun, but that's impossible now, with Zachary, with my job."

"Have kid and computer, can't travel?" Ryan asked, taking Janna's hand again, giving it a small squeeze. She was putting on a bright face but he could tell, as only the child of often-absent parents can, that the long separations bothered her.

"They were on a dig in India when I was born, which explains my name. Janna means Paradise, which is nice, isn't it? Mary—she always wanted me to call her Mary, just like Sam wants me to call him Sam—just gave birth, wrapped me in some sack and put me on her back, and kept on digging. Very dedicated, both Sam and Mary. Very dedicated."

"And you traveled with them? I have to admit I'm jealous. All that travel, all that history—the excitement of discovery."

"Really? Try kneeling on a bunch of sharp gravel in 110 degrees in Egypt for six hours, sifting sand through a sieve, or using a small paintbrush to carefully brush away dirt around an ancient jug in some remote spot in Russia, a jug that turns out to be made in China, and not rare or old or even in one piece. It ain't all romance, as they say,'' she ended, wrinkling up her nose.

They fell silent as they continued down the fairly steep incline, still holding hands. Ryan stole a look at Janna, not really able to see her profile beneath the floppy brim of her hat, and thinking about this very different, very interesting woman.

An unusual, to say the least, childhood. Marriage to an artist. An artist herself, but one with a strong streak of common sense that told her that putting food on her son's plate was more important than being ''true'' to that art. A young widow, making it on her own, and yet still a free spirit. Happy. Outwardly uncomplicated, but with so much inside, so much hidden from view.

And no wonder she was such a good mother to Zachary. She'd known what it was like to have uninterested parents, a childhood without that so necessary warm and loving presence of a parent who *cared.*

''Oh, look—there's Zach!'' Janna cried out as they left the bright sun for the shadows beneath the tall old oak trees that hid the Confederate camp.

Zachary was standing just outside a small, square stand bearing a sign saying Camp Surgeon, listening to a bearded young man in gray wool trousers, white collarless shirt and suspenders explain the use of a myriad of evil-looking tools spread out on an unrolled, cracked leather case.

''And this,'' the ''surgeon'' was saying, holding up a stomach-clenching small saw with hungry teeth, ''is the bone cutter, used for amputations. There wasn't time for saving limbs, you understand, not in the middle of battle, and certainly not if the surgeon wanted time to save other men who were waiting for his services. At the end of some of the larger battles, the stacks of arms and legs piled up outside the hospital reached to the top of the tent.''

"If Zachary says, *cool,* we're going to have a serious talk with the kid,'' Ryan whispered in Janna's ear.

But Ryan needn't have worried. When the ''surgeon'' finished speaking, Zachary's hand shot up as if he were in the classroom, and he asked the reenactor how many soldiers were injured or died during the Civil War.

"More than in all our other wars combined,'' Ryan said, just a heartbeat before the reenactor could answer. He felt his cheeks grow hot as Janna looked up at him, smiling.

"You really *do* know your history, don't you? And it's just a hobby?''

"Just a hobby,'' Ryan said tightly, probably too quickly.

"Uh-huh,'' Janna said, biting on her bottom lip. "Just a hobby. That's what I say about my art.'' Then she brightened, and not a moment too soon, because Ryan was quickly learning that Janna saw a lot deeper than most people. A lot deeper. "Come on, let's get some rock candy. Then we'll have to get ready for the battle.''

"You two go ahead,'' he said. "I'd like to take a longer look at these surgeon's tools.''

"Okay, meet you back at the top of the hill. It's the best place to watch the battle,'' Janna said, then grabbed Zachary's hand and off they went, her boots making an easy passage over damp leaves and tree roots, her silly straw hat flapping in the breeze.

Although he was already standing in the shade, suddenly Ryan felt chilled. Alone. He shook himself, then turned his attention to a small, dark metal thing that looked like a buttonhook...and whose use, he found out moments later, wasn't quite so mundane.

He became so interested in the various booths that were set up to resemble, in some way, a Confederate encampment that the first shot of the cannon took him very much by surprise. He thanked the man he'd been speaking to, then ran back up the hill, looking for Janna and Zachary as the cannon boomed, one after the other, "softening up the enemy" before the foot soldiers made their charge.

He found Zach standing with the Union Army, a drum hanging at his waist, a Union blue hat on his red head, and a wide grin on his face. "Hiya, Mr. Chandler. I've been commandeered, or shanghaied, or whatever it is George said. I'm to get shot almost right away, right in front of all the ladies. It's a real tearjerker, George says."

Ryan lifted his hands, wondering if he should put up some sort of protest, then grinned. "Go for it, buddy. And don't forget to grimace, and kick your legs a time or two once you fall. There could be a movie deal in this for you, you know. Now, where's your mother?"

"You'll see," Zach said, then marched off with the others, who were lining up behind the row of cannon.

Smoke from the cannon tinged the air blue, made it smell of sulfur. The encouraging yells of the foot soldiers as the cannon roared, and belched, and roared again, mingling with the shouts of the "officers" and the growing swell of Rebel yells coming from what Ryan now thought of as "the hollow," had the intended effect of making his heart beat faster, his blood run hotter.

This was war. This was the worst of war, the best of it—if one measured war in valor, and not dead drummer boys and lost dreams.

Above him, on the crest of the hill, a soldier stood spread-legged in the tower, waving a huge red flag until a single gunshot, seemingly louder than the rest, cut him down. They were always the main target, Ryan remembered, wondering if *he* would have had the courage to volunteer for such a dangerous job.

And then there was no more time to think. The Rebel yells split the air and a small sea of gray uniforms broke from shelter along a fifty-foot stretch of trees and began running straight up the hill. Straight toward the cannon, the yawning mouths of death that awaited them.

Just as both armies had done, time and time again, at Vicksburg, at Mission Ridge, at Gettysburg, at Antietam…

The Union Infantry yelled as loud as they could, then set up in two rows, their rifles belching smoke, first in the front kneeling row, then from the second.

Gray uniforms littered the ground, and the bearded man in the white shirt ran out into the middle of the battle, pulling one of the injured back toward the trees before he, too, was cut down.

It was fake. It was a few dozen men wearing blue and gray, garbologists and dentists and factory workers and teachers, putting on a very small show, a miniature of a war that had nearly split the nation.

And it was impressive as hell. Blood chilling, yet exciting. Awful, but fascinating.

History.

Out of the corner of his eye, Ryan saw the moment when Zachary was "hit." The boy dropped his drumsticks, clutched his chest, and began staggering to and fro, moaning. And then, just when Ryan was thinking the kid was overacting, Zachary fell to his knees, then pitched sideways on the ground and lay still. A little redheaded boy, not yet in his teens, dead in the service of his country.

History.

At last, the Confederate Army retreated, carrying off their dead and wounded, and the Union Army rejoiced in its victory—which figured, as this was Pennsylvania, not Georgia, Ryan thought with a wry smile.

And still he hadn't found Janna...until he watched the Union Army reassemble, rifles smartly at their shoulders, and march past the audience. In the second row, third man in, was Janna, her mop of burnished curls sticking out from under a Union hat, her long legs encased in blue, a red stripe down the side of her wool trousers, her face smudged with dirt from the flash powder used in her rifle, her step long and faintly swaggering.

And wearing a grin as wide as all outdoors.

Ryan threw back his head and laughed and laughed. If it was possible to fall in love with a smudged-faced woman in combat boots, he believed he might just have bitten the proverbial dust....

Once again neck-deep in bubble bath, Janna thought back over the day she and Zachary and Ryan had spent at the Reenactment.

It had been fun, of course, but Janna was accustomed to enjoying herself. She'd long ago decided that either she was a basically happy person or she was just easily amused. Either way, she expected to enjoy herself, and that, she'd also decided long ago, was usually half the battle.

But today had been somehow different. More charged with energy, energy she felt radiating toward her from Ryan. His hand in hers. His shoulder brushing against hers. Their easily matched, long strides as they seemed to move together with such an easy grace that anyone would think they'd been walking together for all of their lives.

He'd really enjoyed himself; she was also sure of that. He'd unbent quickly, forgetting that he was the big businessman out of his depth in a grassy field, surrounded by families and reenactors and watching where he stepped so he wouldn't bring home an unwanted souvenir deposited by one of the horses.

But the best, the very best, and the most puzzling, were the purchases Ryan made on the way back down the hill to the parking lot, as they'd stopped at one of the makeshift stands. There had been dozens and dozens of books about the Civil War, about the people, the battles, the politics. Janna had thought he might buy one, just for show, just to prove he was interested.

But he had fooled her. He'd bought three, and had told the bookseller that, no, he didn't need several of the others the man showed him—because he already had them in his personal library.

That shocked Janna. Yes, he had said American history was his hobby—but the books he'd bought, the ones he already owned, seemed to speak of more than just a "hobby."

The bookseller must have sensed the same thing, because he pulled a small, ragged book from under the counter and handed it to Ryan; the personal diary

of a Union soldier, handwritten, and bought by the
man at a recent auction.

Ryan had to have it, and didn't even haggle over
price. He held the book, touched it lovingly, stroking
the cover, carefully turning a few pages…his green
eyes so warm with emotion, Janna had to look away
as it was so intense.

Ryan's hadn't been the look of a collector, someone who wanted *things* just because those things were
available, he had the cash to pay for them, and they
showed him to be an intellectual or something icky
like that.

Oh, no. This was more. Much more. Ryan looked
as if he were holding *history,* and that he was nearly
overwhelmed with the wonder of it.

What was a man like this doing running a clothing
manufacturing plant?

Janna blew some bubbles off her hand, then grimaced. What was a woman like her doing designing
web pages for sprocket manufacturers?

Did she and Ryan have anything in common?
Hopes? Dreams?

Janna sighed. She'd like to believe they did.

Chapter Seven

Ryan came home from work early on Monday. He carried a stuffed briefcase with him, but he laid it on a bench in the foyer and pretty much forgot it as he went in search of Zachary.

The kid had gotten to him, there was no question about that. The way he had smiled up at him from the ground, before "resurrecting" himself from his valiant "death" on the battlefield. The way he had unselfconsciously slipped his hand into Ryan's as they had walked back down the hill toward the car, asking him questions, telling him stories...and generally chattering like a magpie, completely unimpressed by Ryan as anything other than a "guy."

Although Ryan knew he had slipped a notch or two in the boy's admiration—was it really admiration? And why did that feel so *good?*—when he had to admit that he knew next to nothing about soccer.

Which was why he'd come home early today.

He hunted for Zachary through the house, finally

finding him in the backyard, helping his mother put up a swing.

A tire swing, no less. A hunk of rope, an old truck tire. Hanging from a thick branch on a limb of the maple tree Allie had planted years ago, when in one of her rare domestic ''fits'' that had a lot to do with planning and not much to do with actually getting her hands dirty.

But that didn't mean that Allie didn't take great pride in her garden, as she called the nearly full acre of land behind the house. She adored her pool; she lived for her tennis court. She admired all the lovely flowers.

Somehow, Ryan thought with an inward wince, a used truck tire swing just didn't seem to be something Allie would get all cracked up over, esthetically.

''Hello, there!'' he called out as he came down the steps from the terrace, waving. ''I can see Jane, but where's Tarzan?''

''Jane''—the redheaded version—scrunched up her face as she tied one last knot, then smiled at him. ''Want to hear my Tarzan yell?'' she asked. ''It's a beaut.''

''Don't do it! Don't do it!'' Zachary warned Ryan, waving his arms frantically. ''I think it hurts dog ears.''

''Only the persnickety ones,'' Janna scoffed, rubbing her son's head. ''Have a good day in the mines?'' she then asked Ryan, who was pulling on the rope, testing its strength.

''There's good days?'' he answered, pretty much without thinking, then inwardly flinched as Janna leaned closer, peering into his eyes.

She was looking her usual self today, he'd already

noted. Hair on top of her head, like some bright-red mushroom cloud. Jeans hugging her long legs, this time jeans decorated around the hem with colorful embroidery. Combat boots. And another one of those damn sweaters she must have shrunk in the washer. This one was purple, with yellow kitten faces on it.

"You don't like your work?" she asked as he looked away, blinded by her brightness in the sunny afternoon, her seeming ease in looking straight inside of him.

"Who does?" he answered, then gave the rope one last tug. "Zach? Are you ready to try this thing out? Because I don't think this is about to become a permanent fixture around here."

"Why not?" Zachary asked, already inserting himself, rump first, inside the tire. "Allie says she had one when she was a kid. That's why we went home and got this one. Oh," he added, extricating himself from the rump-eating tire, "I forgot. She said she wanted to be the first to swing on it. Gotta go get her."

Ryan watched Zachary run off, then turned to look at Janna. He felt, suddenly, like a stuffed shirt in his tie and three-piece suit, his highly polished wingtips. He reached up and loosened his tie. "So, Allie's okayed this?"

Janna sat down inside the swing and began pushing at the ground with the toe of one boot. "Sure. You didn't think I'd do it without her okay, did you? Zach and I were dunking cookies in milk after he came home from school, when Allie came upstairs to visit. We started talking, she started dunking along with us, and the next thing I knew I was driving home to get the swing. Your grandmother's a hoot, you know. Zach's already madly in love with her.''

Ryan did his best to ignore Janna's last statement. It was natural for his grandmother to be nice to their guests, and a foregone conclusion that she'd be thrilled with Zachary. But investigating Allie's motives in coming upstairs in the first place probably wouldn't make him happy. After all, he was not going to forget that it had been Allie who had picked Janna to bid on him at the bachelor auction.

He smiled at Janna, watching as she tried to gain some height with her kicks, then walked behind her, to give her some helpful pushes. Soon she was flying high in the air, her long legs extended in front of her, her head flung back so that she could grin up at him as he got ready to give her another push.

"Look at me, Ryan! I'm flying!'' she called out, her body lying almost horizontal across the inside rim of the tire. "I've always wanted to be Peter Pan.''

"Not Wendy?'' Ryan asked as she glided back toward him in her next high arc. He grabbed on to the edges of the tire, held her in place as he looked down at her, as she looked up at him.

"Nope. Peter. Definitely Peter. Or maybe Tinkerbell. 'If you *really* believe…''' she quoted, then was gone again, kicking her way through the air, her toes reaching up toward the stars—or at least toward the terrace.

Ryan grabbed at the tire again, slowing her down as he reminded her that Allie was supposed to have the first ride. She nodded her agreement, dragging her boots across the grass when he let her go, letting the swing slowly come to a stop, the truck tire beginning a slow spin.

"We'd better make a break for it, before they get here," Janna teased, grabbing his hand and heading for the garages. "The tire might still be warm, and give us away."

Ryan laughed, and followed along, especially since he'd heard the roar of a badly in-need-of-a-tuneup engine coming from the driveway. "That's the delivery truck I was expecting," he said when Janna saw the van in the driveway and looked at Ryan for an explanation. After all, it couldn't be every day that a van carrying the painted words Bill's Sporting Goods showed up in the Chandler driveway.

"What's this?" she asked as two men pulled a huge box from the back doors of the van.

"Basketball hoop. For Zachary, so he doesn't get bored here after school. Fiberglass back, NBA approved. With its own stand and everything," Ryan answered proudly, pulling a few bills from his pocket and handing them to the men. "They'll have it up in no time," he added, stepping back beside Janna.

"*They'll* have it up? Oh, no. That's half the joy of something new, Ryan, putting it together. And I'll help. Zach, too."

Ryan looked at Janna, looked at the huge box. Remembered what the hoop and stand had looked like, set up, inside the sporting goods shop. He tried to be tactful. "Put this thing together ourselves? Are you— let's see, what's the word I'm looking for? Oh, I know—are you *nuts?*"

"There's always that possibility," Janna answered, already pushing up the sleeves of her sweater. "You probably should go get a screwdriver or something. Come on, it'll be fun."

And it was fun for, oh, about fifteen minutes.

Zach's bug-eyed response to learning the hoop was
for him had carried Ryan through uncrating the
pieces. The boy's enthusiasm in setting out the pieces,
comparing them with the list found inside the box,
was even a little infectious.

But when Janna began reading the directions? That
was just about when the bloom began leaving this
particular rose. "We'll need," she told him, "two
people—got that, plus one, or at least a half-a-people.
A tape measure, some tape, a hammer, a couple of
wrenches—you do have wrenches, don't you?—a
piece of scrap wood, a stepladder. And sand or a garden hose, to weight down the base so it won't tip.
Oh, this is going to be *great* once it's up."

Maybe. But not until Zachary deserted them for the
swing, and Ryan and Janna made a trip to the local
hardware store on the hunt for a "9/16 inch deep
socket wrench w/Ext. is recommended," among other
things.

On the way home from the store, with a stepladder
hanging half out of the window, Janna said, "I still
can't believe you guys have no tools. How do you
survive?"

Ryan stopped at a red light and all but glared at
her. "You hired me as your handyman and I damn
near burned down your house. Now, just imagine, if
you will, what I could do armed with a nine-sixteenth-
inch wrench."

"Point taken," Janna said, giggling. "Does it
bother you? Being so mechanically inept, that is?"

"Only when you bring it up," Ryan growled, stepping on the gas once more. "We've always just hired
someone. I never even thought about it before, to tell
you the truth. So, now that you finally realize the full

extent of my incompetence, when do you think we'll have the hoop up—June?''

Janna reached over and patted his cheek. "Oh, ye of little faith. I, through necessity and not a little natural talent, am extremely mechanically minded. We'll have it up in a couple of hours, and because there are spotlights outside the garages, you'll even be able to impress the heck out of Zachary with your great three-point shot.''

Ryan nearly rear-ended the car in front of them. "How...how did you know?"

Janna grinned, wiggled around a little in her seat. "I'm brilliant? No, that can't be it. Let me see...oh, okay, I have it. Zach was bummed when you didn't know anything about soccer, so you decided to show him something you *did* know something about—basketball. Or did you get through high school with that towering height without the basketball coach grabbing you by the ear in the hallway and telling you to come out for the team? I sure didn't.''

He decided to ignore her on-target deductions. "You played basketball in high school?"

"Correction. I played basketball for *three* high schools. Sam and Mary moved around a lot, remember? I was a real big hit on the Isle of Capri, I can tell you. The fans called me their *rosso chiaro*—that means *bright red*, because my hair was even more like Zach's is now, brighter, you know, until I got a little older. And I have to tell you, my set shot is *so* sweet...."

He heard the challenge in her voice, saw the delicious mischief in her eyes. "You're on, Red," he said, turning into the driveway. "One game of Horse. I'll even let you shoot first. Deal?"

She held out her hand to him. "Deal," she said, shaking his hand, holding it. "Just don't think I'm going to cut you any breaks, because I won't."

"Same here," Ryan said solemnly, feeling the heat of Janna's slim hand in his, realizing that, for all her height, her bones were as fragile as any woman's. Her skin whiter and softer than most. He gave a slight tug on her hand, pulling her closer to him in the car.

Closer.

"Janna?" he asked, looking at her mouth.

Closer.

"Yes?" she answered, her voice no longer mocking, but slightly tremulous.

Closer.

"Hey! You guys coming or what?" Zachary yelled, banging on the driver's side window, and the mood was broken.

After dinner, and after Ryan had two new bandages—one on his left thumb, one on his right index finger—and after a sometimes heated discussion as to the rules of Horse, Janna and Ryan faced each other on the driveway.

Allie, Mrs. Ballantine, Joe and Maddy—who'd popped popcorn—Matt and Jessica—who already had the bowl sitting in her lap—and Zachary made up the spectators, sitting on lawn chairs along the grass edging the driveway.

"She's going first? Well, that's gentlemanly, at least," Allie said, reaching into the bowl of popcorn. "Now, Matt, tell me the rules again, please."

Matt, no stranger to the basketball court himself, sat back in his chair, crossing one long leg over the other. "It's simple, Allie. Two players or more—in this case, just two. Anyway, the first guy takes a shot, from wherever he wants, and the second guy has to take his shot from the same place. If the first guy hits and the second guy hits, they move on, take the next shots from a different spot. However, if the first guy hits and the second guy misses, the second guy gets a letter from the word *horse*.''

"But if the *first* guy misses," Joe interjected, "then the second guy can pick any spot at all to shoot from, and if he makes the shot, the first shooter gets a letter from the word horse. The first person to spell *horse* loses.''

"Just horse?" Allie asked, her grin wicked. "Not horse's a—''

"Allie! Shame on you!" Maddy interrupted, laughing.

"Can we get back to the rules?" Matt asked, shaking his head. "Well, I already told you the rules. Now I'll tell you the strategy. The *secret* is for both guys to know their own strengths, and the other guy's weaknesses, then place themselves for shots easy for them, hard for the other guy. Understand?''

"Not even vaguely, darling," Allie said, popping a handful of popcorn into her mouth. "But, please, don't feel the need to explain it all to me again. I think I'll be happier in my ignorance.''

"Which explains why she's been near to delirious her whole life long," Mrs. Ballantine mumbled, earning a giggle from Maddy, who was the only one who'd heard her.

"Go, Mom!" Zachary shouted from the sidelines, punching a fist into the air as Janna took up a position at the top of the key and went into her stance.

"Awright!" he yelled when the ball hit nothing but net.

Janna turned to her son, took a bow, then grabbed the bouncing ball and handed it to Ryan.

Now it was his turn.

"You're loving this, aren't you?" he asked, and Janna, who'd never quite seen the reasoning behind little white lies, answered, "Straight down to my toes, big boy. And remember, we've got rules. No cheating."

"How could I cheat?" Ryan asked.

"How? Well, horse is spelled with *one R,* for starters. And don't say you've never pulled that trick, because I won't believe you. We've *all* done it, so I'll be keeping track along with you."

He blushed. Right here, right now, in the light from the spotlights, the man blushed. And Janna, being Janna, stood up on tiptoes and gave him a kiss on the cheek. "Don't worry. Zach is crazy about you, win or lose."

Then she stood back, tried not to look into his expressive green eyes, and wondered why it suddenly felt as if her heart had relocated in her throat.

"Come on, Ryan, and don't let her sweet-talk you into throwing the game," Matt called out encouragingly. "Piece of cake, you can do it."

And do it Ryan did. A clean shot. Nothing but net.

While Joe and Matt laid ridiculous side bets, and Allie and Jessica fought over the popcorn, the game went on. And on.

After a dozen sets of shots, Janna had H-O.

Ryan had H-O-R.

And Allie was having the time of her life.

"Did you see that, Lucille? Did you, did you?"

she demanded of Mrs. Ballantine. "She sank that one while facing *away* from the basket!"

"I'm only sorry we didn't get it on tape with the video camera," the housekeeper drawled sarcastically, getting to her feet, then bending down to whisper in Allie's ear. "They're a perfect match, Almira. And, before you pat yourself on the back, I don't think you had a thing to do with it. Now, I'm going inside for a cup of tea."

Allie waved her away, then looked at Janna, who was waiting for Ryan to take his shot. Dear girl. Strange girl, but a dear girl. They might not look a thing alike, but Allie was more than a little certain that, somehow, she had found a woman for Ryan who had been cut from the same bolt of cloth as herself. Fine linen for herself, something wildly tie-dyed for Janna—but Allie knew what she meant.

A strong-willed woman. An independent woman. A woman with a huge capacity for love, for laughter.

And, she conceded to herself—and never to anyone else—this was one time when Lucille was right. It was time she backed off, and let nature take its course. She'd never thought that day would arrive, sometimes worried that it never would…but suddenly she realized that it was all right. The world could turn without her personal vigilance. Her dearest children *could* muddle through without her.

And it felt good. Really, really good.

"Come on, Ryan!" she shouted, cupping her hands around her mouth. "Hit it out of the park!"

"That's baseball, Allie," Joe told her, laughing. "But I think he gets the idea. Yep—nothing but net. This could go on for hours."

"Or years," Allie said, smiling. "Even decades. Isn't that nice?"

Ryan sat on a stool in Janna's galley kitchen, wiping his face with a towel she'd thrown to him. "You let me win."

Janna poured two glasses of ice water and placed one in front of him on the breakfast bar, avoiding his eyes. "I did not," she lied, glad Zach had already gone to bed. "And I can't imagine how I missed that last shot, considering I try to get into a pickup game at the park at least once a week. How long has it been since you've played?"

Ryan leaned over, rubbed at his aching shins. "Too long," he told her, knowing he'd probably be walking like an eighty-year-old man by the next morning. "And now Zach wants me to show him how to dribble. Hell, if I don't get some sleep, I'll only be able to show him how to *drool*."

Janna laughed out loud, circling around the bar and sitting down on the stool next to his. "You're very good, you know. You really should keep playing, if just for the exercise. Why did you stop? You said you played in high school. Didn't you play in college, too?"

Ryan turned away from her, stretched out his legs. "Not in college, no. I carried two majors, one in business, the other in history. I didn't have time for extracurricular activities. As it was, I shouldn't have taken on the history major."

"Why not, if you were interested in it?" Janna asked, looking at him, seeing him vulnerable in his khakis and open-collared knit shirt. Seeing him as a little boy, like her Zach. A little boy with dreams…and a grown man who had put those dreams aside. The only question was: why?

"Mother and Dad had died, and I had to get through school, take over the reins of the business so my grandfather could retire. I almost made it, too," he said, looking at her. "But then my grandfather had his first stroke, and I was in it with both feet. There hasn't been a lot of time for much of anything else since then, even with Jessica helping me. And now she's told me she's going to quit soon, and raise her family full-time. I don't mind. I mean, she's making the right choice. But some of us don't have choices," he concluded, picking up his glass, looking into it as if it might contain the answer to some unanswerable question.

"We all have choices, Ryan," Janna said, putting her elbows on the bar and cupping her chin in her hands. "Why don't you think you do?"

He smiled at her, but it was a sad smile, and she felt this sudden urge to move closer, put her arms around him, comfort him. And more. And *not* because Almira Chandler had thought she'd do a good job of it, or whatever it was Almira Chandler had thought that first night. Janna *liked* Ryan. She really, really liked him. Maybe more than liked him, which was strange and yet wonderful, for she hadn't felt like this about a man since she'd met Mark…so many years ago. "What would your choice be, if you had a choice?"

"Teaching," Ryan said on a sigh. He actually looked embarrassed. "American history, actually, which is taught in the ninth grade around here. But life intrudes on dreams sometimes, doesn't it? Not that I'm complaining. We have a very good family business, and I'm very good at running it for the family. So," he said, swiveling on his stool, standing up, "that's that. Confession time's over. Now, if you'll excuse me, I think I have a date with a hot shower and probably some aspirin."

Janna unbent her long limbs from around the legs of her own stool, and slid to her feet. Putting a hand on Ryan's forearm, holding him in place, she said, "Teaching, huh? You know, I think you'd make a fabulous teacher. I know you already have Zach eating out of your hand. He said you know more about the Civil War than George, and make it more interesting, too—and that's high praise."

"Zach's a great kid," Ryan said, putting his own hand on top of Janna's, making her stomach do a nifty little flip that also had its place in her memory, but one she hadn't felt in much too long a time.

"And you're a nice man," she told him honestly. "A very, very nice man." Taking a breath, taking a chance, she stood up on tiptoe and pressed her mouth against his.

She fit against him so well. Did he notice?

His mouth was so warm, so firm yet soft. So gentle; undemanding, yet making her want to give him anything he asked. All he had to do was say the word, and she was his.

His arms went around her, drawing her closer as his lips slanted against hers, moved against hers, encouraged her to open her own lips, let him inside.

She pressed her hands against the back of his shoulders, felt his hands splay over her lower back, her buttocks, so that they both were vitally aware of each other, the physical effect they had on each other.

Ryan's hands began to stray. He couldn't help himself, couldn't stop himself. And Janna didn't fight him.

She simply accepted him, as if this was so right, so natural. She was a giver. She gave her smiles, her laughter, her warm heart. And she didn't seem to want anything back from him except that which he freely gave.

And took. He was in danger of taking too much. Too much, too soon.

The thought sobered him.

Ryan broke off the embrace, kissed the tip of her nose, and took a deep breath. "Lots of different definitions of *fire*, aren't there?" he said rather breathlessly. "But I think I've burned down enough kitchens for one week. Good night, Janna."

"Good night, Ryan," she said, putting her hands on her hips, looking at him, enjoying the view. "Want to come to the house with me tomorrow, to check on the progress? I can't believe you've got two crews working already."

He seemed to hesitate for a moment, then agreed.

"Good," she answered, grinning. "And we can bury the cat clock. Zachary's already written a small eulogy, although I never knew so many words rhymed with *blue*."

The tension eased, as she'd meant it to do. Ryan laughed, saluted and left the kitchen, the small apartment. Leaving Janna to sit down at the breakfast bar again, her bottom lip caught between her teeth, and wonder where all of this could be leading, if it would actually lead anywhere.

She knew what she hoped.

What, she wondered, did Ryan hope?

Chapter Eight

Tuesday, after school, and with Ryan finding yet another excuse to leave work early, they buried the cat.

Janna had been right. Ryan also hadn't realized just how many words rhymed with *blue,* although how Zach had worked *kangaroo* into the third verse of the rhymed eulogy was still, thankfully, rather fuzzy in his mind.

Wednesday, he'd come home to find Janna in the main kitchen with Maddy, teaching her how to make homemade granola cereal. He'd grabbed one of Allie's favorite powdered doughnuts and escaped the kitchen, finding Zachary in the backyard, already waiting with the basketball under his arm.

Thursday, they dropped Zachary at soccer practice, and went to see the house again.

The contractor was making rapid progress, a fact that brought a quick frown to Ryan's face before he remembered he wanted nothing more than for the house repairs to be completed and Janna back where she belonged, his *mind* back where it belonged, on business.

That made him frown even more, because he'd pretty much decided where Janna and Zachary belonged, and it wasn't here, in this small Cape Cod house.

Not while he was in the large, rambling Chandler house, on his own.

The workers had left for the day, leaving behind some tools in the kitchen, a pile of charred wallboard and other garbage in a rented Dumpster in the backyard, and the remnants of somebody's fast-food lunch.

Janna pocketed her key as Ryan closed the kitchen door behind them, and tiptoed her way through the work area, tipping her head this way and that, trying to imagine the completed job.

"It's going to be fine, just fine," she said, more to make Ryan feel better than to convince herself. After all, she knew the kitchen would be repaired. She knew she could redecorate it, pick other colors for the walls, sew up new curtains, select another table and chairs. Another clock.

That wasn't the problem. Decorating was *fun*. The problem, she knew, was that she simply couldn't find any enthusiasm for the project, no matter how deeply she dug inside herself.

So, naturally, she threw herself into waxing nearly poetic over the changes she'd make in the room. "What do you think, Ryan? Yellow? Yellow's so sunny and warm, probably perfect for a kitchen. Although not if you're hung over, and groping for the aspirin while squinting against all that happy, sunny yellow."

"You planning on being hung over much?" Ryan asked, picking up Tansy's dish, reminding himself to remember to take it back to the house when they left. Not that it bothered him that the cat was currently drinking water out of a particularly expensive bit of Waterford crystal. Really. It didn't bother him at all. He even thought it was rather funny. But that didn't mean Maddy would, if she ever visited her old apartment.

"Me? Hung over? Not really, no. Oh, I did it— once—when I was a freshman in college, and decidedly underage. But once was more than enough, and I plan never to do it again. Isn't it funny how we can want to do something so badly when we're not supposed to, then find out it loses all its appeal once we're *allowed* to do it?"

"The lure of the forbidden," Ryan said, then looked at Janna as she bent to pick up a discarded French fry container. Extraordinarily limber, she bent from the waist, like a dancer, and his gaze lingered on her body until he reminded himself of his own statement: the lure of the forbidden.

Yeah? And so whose army had posted No Trespassing signs anyway, huh?

Janna wadded up the paper container and pitched it neatly into a cardboard box already half-filled with various garbage. "I think whât I need to do is go shopping. Then, once I find something I like, I can sort of *build* the rest of the room around it. That's how I did it the first time, with the cat clock."

"And inspiring it was, too," Ryan said, trying to keep a straight face. "Just do me a favor, and don't fall in love with leopard-design table mats. It wouldn't take a hangover to send someone screaming from the kitchen if you did that.''

"Leopard-design place mats?'' Janna pretended to consider this. ''Naw, you're right. It might be just a little too *much,* you know? Shall we go check on the rest of the house? I need to dig up some more underwear for Zachary anyway. He's gone from terminally cruddy to taking two showers a day. I'd like to think he's discovered personal hygiene, but I think it has more to do with the shower in the apartment. Did you know it has six nozzles? I'm half in love with that shower myself, although I'm also partial to the old claw-footed tub.''

A quick, painful vision of Janna standing in the black-tile-lined shower in Maddy's old apartment, water jets pulsing at her from six different heights and directions actually had Ryan feeling light-headed for a moment. But he recovered quickly, or at least he hoped he did. ''Yes, the rest of the house. Let's do it.''

Janna tipped her head, looked at Ryan for a few moments, wondering if the man knew he was flushed, clear to his hairline. Oh, he was just *so* cute!

She stopped in the dining room, to inspect the mural. ''You know,'' she said, touching a finger to the wall, ''this isn't as great as I thought it was. There's definitely smoke damage.'' She sighed, shrugged her shoulders. ''I think it has to go.''

Ryan touched the wall as well, placing his fingers on Janna's painted profile, tracing them along the wall until he touched on Zachary's smiling face. ''Are you sure? Can't it be saved?''

''Things change, Ryan. We have to change along with them. The mural was nice, and I enjoyed it every day. Now I'll get to enjoy something else. It was only a *thing,* remember. I still have Zach, and I'll always have the memory of this mural. It's enough.''

Ryan's glance landed on the inexpensive pine sideboard painted a soft moss green, and the dozen or more photographs that sat there. ''We could take pictures first,'' he suggested, walking around the small round dining table to pick up a silver-framed photograph of a smiling young man who had to be Mark.

He held the picture in his hand, seeing bits of Zachary around his father's eyes, a hint of the boy in the man's smile. ''He looks like a very nice man.''

Janna joined him at the sideboard, looking down at the picture with him. ''He was a wonderful man,'' she agreed softly. ''A wonderful, wonderful man.''

''And now you have your memories,'' Ryan said, feeling stabs of pain he knew he shouldn't feel, but unable to stop them from piercing his chest, his heart. ''How did he...I mean, what...never mind. I shouldn't ask.''

''How did Mark die?'' Janna took the picture from Ryan, pressed two fingers to her lips, then to the glass, then carefully put the frame back down on the sideboard. ''It's all right to ask. I don't mind. Let's go upstairs and raid Zach's underwear drawer while we talk, okay?''

Following along like an obedient child, Ryan listened as Janna talked.

''Zach was only a baby at the time. Eighteen months—but I think I already told you that,'' she said, her voice low, but clear. ''Mark was holding him, actually, after I was through feeding him. And then suddenly Mark was yelling for me to take Zach. Holding his hands to his head, screaming with pain...just screaming with the pain. Then...then he just sort of...fell over.''

Ryan tried to imagine a young wife's terror, the terror of a young mother. ''Brain tumor?'' he asked quietly, as Janna rooted through the bottom drawer of Zachary's bureau.

All right, Janna realized, so maybe talking about Mark wasn't going to be as easy as she'd believed, especially as it felt so important to her that Ryan *understand* how she'd felt about Mark, how she felt today, and would tomorrow, and for the rest of her life.

So she momentarily changed the subject. ''I kept Zach's underwear in the lowest drawer so he could reach it. Now he's almost ten, and shows signs of being taller than either Mark or me, and we're still keeping the underwear in the bottom drawer. Silly, isn't it?''

Then she stood up, faced Ryan, said what had to be said. ''No, not a brain tumor.'' She went into the hallway and took a large plastic bag from the hall linen closet, stuffing the clothing inside. ''It was a brain aneurysm. Several of them, as a matter of fact. Mark had been born with them, time bombs ticking in his head. One of them just...popped. They operated immediately...but he never regained consciousness, although he hung on for another two weeks.'' Her smile was watery, and she knew it. ''I had time to say goodbye.''

Ryan shook his head, trying to picture Janna's grief, imagine her terror and fear for the future. ''How did you manage it? A young woman and a baby, alone in New York....''

''Oh, Sam and Mary came and stayed for a while,'' Janna said, now heading into her office, because she couldn't stand still, didn't want to stand still. "We managed, although it took some fast talking to convince Sam I couldn't just load Zach on my back and go off on a dig to Chile with them. I even stayed on at the loft for a few years, determined not to change anything, determined to keep Mark's dream alive. But it was Mark's dream, not mine, and I finally realized that. A person doesn't need a loft in the Village to create web pages."

"So you closed your eyes, cheated a little and moved here, to Allentown?"

She smiled. "You remember that? Yes, that's what we did. And now I have my memories, and they're just fine. Just fine."

"And *you're* fine, too?"

Janna picked up a bronze paperweight in the shape of a dolphin, put it down again in much the same spot. "Yes," she said, turning to look at Ryan, tears standing in her eyes even as she smiled. "I'm fine, too." She hesitated a moment, then continued, "I really didn't have much choice, did I? I had a child to raise, my memories, and the sure knowledge that Mark would kick my butt straight out of heaven once I got there if I hadn't gone on with my life. Because life is a gift, isn't it, Ryan? Not really living that gift...well, it's almost criminal. I still have my art, and if there's still time for it later, maybe I'll go back to it. For now, however, I'm going to enjoy the gifts I have."

Ryan stepped forward, cupped Janna's chin, and softly kissed her mouth. "You're an extraordinary woman, Janna Monroe. And I wish I had your guts...er, your courage. To really live your life, that is."

"And you don't? Why?" As Ryan began to turn away, she grabbed his arm, pulled him back to face her. "You're talking about your dream of teaching, aren't you? And more. You're saying—without saying—that you don't like the life you're living now. You know, I still don't get it. If you want to teach, teach. If you want to jump off a bridge without a parachute, well, then maybe you ought to rethink the idea. But to teach? Why not, for crying out loud? Why keep doing something that obviously doesn't make you happy? That's—well, that's *dumb.*"

Ryan looked at her for a long moment, then just said, "Thank you."

She didn't say, "You're welcome," because he was already walking away. And, she knew, he was going away mad.

It was amazing how cool the weather could turn after so many unseasonably warm days in a row. But cool it was, especially when Janna and Ryan encountered each other in the main part of the house.

Ryan was subtle. He'd say hello, then make some excuse to leave the room.

Janna was Janna. She'd stand her ground, then stick her tongue out at him as he went.

Three days after their confrontation at the damaged house, Janna was standing in the drawing room as Ryan excused himself yet again, when Allie asked, "Lovers' spat, my dear? Or shouldn't I be so hopeful?"

Janna walked across the drawing room and flopped down on the sofa behind the low table already laid for tea. She'd been handed a standing invitation—"command"—to have tea each day at four with Allie, who definitely enjoyed playing her role of matriarch. And, thanks to Mrs. Ballantine's warning, Janna pretty much knew why *she* had been ordered to these daily "command performances."

Still, she thought she'd try now to get Allie to clarify her reasons.

"Hopeful that we're fighting, or hopeful that it's a lovers' spat, Allie?" she asked, picking up a homemade oatmeal-and-raisin cookie and biting off half of it with an energy usually reserved for belligerent lions ripping off hunks of fresh meat somewhere in the Serengeti. "I'm still trying to figure out if you see me as a lure or as the fish."

"Is that an analogy? Yes, I think maybe it is. At least it's something that has a literary term for it the writer probably never realized while he was scribbling the thing. Very good, Janna. But whatever would make you think I'm a fisherman? No," Allie said, smoothing her knee-length skirt, "I think I'd rather you'd ask if I thought you were the goad or the goal. You see, I could have wanted you around just to remind my grandson that there's a whole life out there he's missing. Or I could have wanted you around because I believe you to be exactly what Ryan needs, for now, and for forever. Do you want to know which it is?"

Janna hesitated in the middle of dumping a third teaspoon of sugar in her tea. "No, not particularly, as it might scare me. But I do love a sneaky woman."

"And my grandson?" Allie prodded. "How do you feel about him?"

"How do you feel about Ryan, Allie?" Janna asked, turning the question right back at the other woman. "Oh, I know you love him. But how else do you see him? Do you, for instance, think he's not happy because he doesn't have a woman in his life? That the answer might be that simple? Or do you think there's more to it than that?''

"It works in my beloved romance novels. Although there are always other problems to solve, not just finding the right mate. I'm surprised I hadn't thought of that." Allie turned her head a little, looked at Janna out of the corners of her eyes. "You know something, don't you? I *knew* you were perfect the moment I laid my eyes on your combat boots! Spill it, girl. Spill your guts."

Janna shook her head, stood. "Nope. Can't. It would be betraying a confidence."

Allie pulled a mock comical face, which wasn't easy, considering the amount of cosmetic surgery she'd had over the past two decades. "Oh, good Lord, don't tell me the silly girl has *scruples!* I guess it's true, then. Nobody's perfect. I, on the other hand, have worked long and hard to avoid scruples. So far, I'm proud to say, it has worked." Allie leaned forward in her seat. "That said, can you give me a hint? I'm serious here, Janna. I'm not blind, I know Ryan is troubled, has been troubled for a long time, but I'll be damned—er, *dipped*—if I've been able to figure it out. I gave you and that boy of yours a roof over your heads, remember. You must owe me something."

"My eternal gratitude?" Janna couldn't help herself, she grinned like a fool, and knew it. Lordy, but she loved sparring with this woman. "My grandmother's recipe for pumpkin bread? A few lessons in calligraphy? Your very own pastel caricature of yourself? That would be a hoot, wouldn't it? I could put a little tennis racket in your one hand, and a witch's broomstick in the other.''

Allie looked at her levelly. ''My grandson isn't speaking to you. Are you sure you can afford having me not speaking to you as well? After all, that would only leave Mrs. Ballantine, and she doesn't speak to anyone. Well, she does, but she never says anything the least interesting or nice. Now, give me that hint, and I'll decide where to go with it.''

Janna stood up, smoothed down her clothing as if she'd just emerged, victorious, from a fistfight, and was willing to be graceful to her vanquished opponent. ''I've seen your bookcases full of romance novels, Allie. They tell me that you're a romantic, a kind woman, a loving woman—even an intelligent woman, for an unintelligent woman wouldn't read. Have you ever checked your grandson's bookshelves? They tell their own story.''

''His book—his *bookshelves?*'' Allie shook her head, trying to understand. ''That's it? That's your hint?''

''And it's enough of a hint, for an intelligent woman like yourself.''

''Ryan's bookshelves are in his apartment. You've been in his apartment?''

''Nope,'' Janna answered brightly. ''But then, he *talked* to me. He's regretting it, that's for sure, but he did talk to me. His bookshelves will talk to you, I promise. Unless you're not allowed in his apartment?''

Allie, who had been sipping the last of her tea, coughed and spluttered and had to cover her mouth with her napkin. ''Not *allowed?* That day will never dawn, my dear!''

"No, I didn't think so," Janna said, then headed for the driveway, as she had seen Ryan and Zachary through one of the French doors from the drawing room, playing one-on-one. She figured they might need a referee…especially once she'd seen Zachary fake Ryan out, then duck between his legs for a layup.

A child after her own heart, her son was, Janna thought as she rubbed her hands together, eager for a little friendly competition. And Ryan would have to stay out there, play along, or else look silly in front of Zach.

Kids came in *so* handy sometimes….

Chapter Nine

Ryan was pacing in his apartment close to midnight, unable to sleep.

Which shouldn't have surprised him. It certainly wouldn't have surprised his grandmother, if he'd told her, but then he was pretty sure he didn't have a death wish, which meant the last, the very *last* person he wanted to talk with right now was Almira Chandler.

Janna was impossible. That was the one conclusion Ryan had been able to come to as he paced. Totally impossible. For one, she didn't play by the rules. Ryan wasn't entirely sure what the rules *were,* but he was damn positive Janna broke them all.

People who have arguments don't talk to each other. That was a given, right?

So why did Janna keep showing up everywhere he was, smiling and laughing, and acting as if she didn't know he was angry with her? They'd fought, hadn't they? Had themselves pretty much of a knock-down-drag-out fight about his supposed lack of guts.

And she'd just about come out and said that. "Ryan, you have no guts." She thought he was an idiot; a gutless idiot.

"If you want something, go get it." That was what she'd told him. "What's the worst that could happen? You fall flat on your face? Well, so what? Just pick yourself up, and go at it again."

Ryan stopped in front of one of his many bookcases and ran his hand across several well-worn book spines. "She just doesn't get it," he told the books, himself, the empty room. "It's not just me, damn it. It's Allie and Maddy and Jess and Mrs. Ballantine and two hundred loyal employees, all of them counting on me. *Me.*"

He pulled out a book, part of a rare, first edition pictorial series on the Civil War, then slammed it back in place. "I can see it now. I call everyone together, tell them I have this *dream,* and that I'm bailing, walking away, following my dream, and I hope they won't mind. Jess can come back to work with a baby on each hip, Maddy can ask Joe for help, and the employees—well, there's always unemployment insurance if it doesn't work out, isn't there. Sure, that'd work."

Flopping his long-legged body into a nearby overstuffed chair he kept for its comfort, not its looks, Ryan dropped his head in his hands and closed his eyes.

Which didn't help.

Because, when he closed his eyes, when he allowed his mind to go blank for more than two seconds, and with every third breath, all he could do was see Janna, think of Janna, breathe in her clean scent that haunted his days and nights.

Their one-on-one basketball game this afternoon hadn't helped, either. Not with Janna guarding him so closely, bumping that long, lithe figure against him, working him with her hip as she lined up a shot, putting her hands on his hips as he tried to fake her out, break free for his own shot.

The woman had twelve hands, she had to. And absolutely no shame. She'd even faked a turned ankle so that he'd relaxed his guard, then flashed past him to the basket, calling out, "Sucker!" as she sank another two-pointer.

He could have killed her. Or kissed her. He'd much preferred to kiss her, except that Zachary was on the sidelines, watching their every move, laughing and calling out encouragement to both of them.

And Ryan had enjoyed himself. In spite of his anger, in spite of his dilemma of wanting to touch Janna and wanting to stay as far from temptation as possible, in spite of the sure knowledge that he was rapidly losing his mind, Ryan had enjoyed himself.

He'd enjoyed himself so much that he'd gone out to dinner on his own, to sulk, and was now wearing a hole in what was a very good antique carpet—feeling sorry for himself, ashamed of himself, and *way* too lonely.

Maybe if he went downstairs, made himself some hot tea, or warm milk…or a double Scotch? He didn't have a kitchen in his smaller apartment, as he'd altered the floor plan because he wanted more living space and didn't really cook anyway. He also didn't drink much besides the occasional beer or glass of wine, so there was no bar, and no Scotch, within easy reach.

So, dressed in an old pair of running shorts with

his college name fading away on one leg, and with a T-shirt that Maddy had brought back from Spain on her month-long honeymoon, Spaniards do it with *olé*—written in both Spanish and English—he headed for the door and the shared landing with the other apartment.

He'd just about gotten the door open when he heard it.

"Eeeooouuuwww! Yooowww! Eeeoowww!"

"What the—" He took two steps in the direction of Janna's apartment, leaned his ear against the door, and heard it again, louder and longer.

Clearly someone was killing someone inside Janna's apartment.

He knocked on the door, ready to break it down if someone didn't answer by the time he counted to five. He was at four when Janna opened the door, then winced as she saw his expression.

"You can hear her, can't you? Oh, I'm so sorry. But there's really nothing I can do about it, you know. Nature is nature."

Ryan shook his head, trying to clear it of the vision of Janna with tousled curls, a thigh-length gray T-shirt with Lehigh University stamped on it; she also wore an ankle-length blue-and-white-striped bathrobe, but as it was hanging open, that didn't much matter anyway. And he used to think he was in a rut, with an uneventful life—and he used to think that was a bad thing.

Now, he wondered about that.

"What are you talking about?" he asked, looking down at her bare feet. Even that was a mistake; Janna had great feet....

The noise came again. Loud, piercing, darn near horrific. *"Eeeooouuuwww! Yooowww! Eeeoowww!"*

"Is that Zach? That can't be Zach."

Janna stepped back from the door, motioning with a sweep of her hand that Ryan should come in, probably so that she could close the door and hopefully not wake up either Allie or Mrs. Ballantine.

"No, silly, it's not Zach. It's Tansy."

"Tansy? Your *cat?* Well, what the hell's wrong with her? Does she have her tail caught in something? Is she sick? I don't get it."

Janna pressed her lips together for a moment, then stood on tiptoe to whisper in Ryan's ear. "She's feeling *amorous*," she said, then added, "and this is one biology class I'm not really ready to hold for Zachary, so please keep your voice *down.*"

"My voice? *My* voice? Tansy's loud enough for all of us," Ryan pointed out, walking into the living room to be immediately approached by the blue-cream cat, who began winding herself around his leg, looking up at him hopefully. "Oh, good," he snarled. "That's really, really good. Just what I needed to make my night complete."

"Oh, don't pout," Janna said as she bent to scoop up the cat. "You should be flattered to know how irresistible you are."

Tansy glared at him balefully, her yellow eyes seemingly reproaching him for not having had the forethought to bring some local tomcat with him when he visited, then jumped down from Janna's arms. She began wailing again, and up-close and personal, it was an earsplitting lament.

"Isn't there anything we can do?" he asked, wishing he'd had the sense to run that sentence past himself silently before opening his mouth and saying something quite so stupid.

"I don't think so, unless you think a cold shower or a copy of the latest centerfold in *Petboy* is available—and, no, I'm kidding. There is no such magazine as *Petboy*. That was supposed to be a joke."

"I knew that," Ryan said, looking down at the cat that was lying on the floor at the moment, looking dangerously calm. "And she knows I'm not a tomcat, right?"

"I think so," Janna offered, trying her best to hold back a giggle, then sobered. "I'm so sorry, Ryan. She's not quite a year old, and I thought we had a couple more months to make up our minds whether to breed her or...or, you know. I won't say it out loud, poor T's upset enough as it is."

As if to prove Janna's statement, Tansy got up, began to pace, and yowl, once more.

"Oh, poor baby," Janna said. "Maybe some milk?"

Ryan followed her into the kitchen. "How long does this go on? I mean, is tonight it, or is there more?"

"I don't know," she answered, then snapped her fingers at him. "The Internet! I'll go check on the Internet. You stay here, pour some milk into her bowl. I'll be right back."

Ryan opened his mouth, lifted his index finger in protest, but Janna was already gone...and Tansy was sitting on the tile floor, looking at him as if he were a piece of fresh meat just thrown into the tiger cage. "Milk, cat," he said forcefully. "You're getting milk, and my wholehearted sympathy—but that's it."

Tansy settled for the milk, a first-time treat for her,

and Ryan went back into the living room, slightly relaxed. He looked around, seeing that Janna had put her stamp on the room in what was beginning to seem to him to be typical Janna fashion.

There was an obviously hand-crocheted throw on the back of the couch: yellow daisies on a bright-green background. Somehow, it went well on the white-on-white-striped satin Queen Anne couch.

She'd brought along a wooden sculpture of some naked goddess, now standing on a marble base, her arms uplifted, reaching for the stars. That sat on the coffee table, right beside a rather impressive-looking coffee table book with a photograph of that same piece on its cover.

Now that was interesting.

He picked up the book, hefted its weight, then saw that the book had been written by Samuel and Mary Frances Monroe. He looked at the photograph. He looked at the statue. Back to the photograph. Back to the statue. He paged through the front of the book, until he found a note on the cover art, explaining that it was fourteenth century, without price, and belonged to the "Monroe Collection."

Monroe? He'd already learned that Janna had kept her maiden name after her marriage, and that she'd done that because Mark had thought she should have some consistency in her name if she was going to seek a future in art. Zach was actually Zachary Monroe-Hastings, carrying both his parents' surnames.

So, taking things to their logical conclusion, this book had to have been written by Janna's parents. Good old Sam and Mary.

Mind-blowing.

He looked at the statue. Priceless, huh? And right

now it was sitting on a coffee table, right next to a half-empty mug of hot chocolate, a ponytail holder looped over one upraised arm and being used as a paperweight to hold down Zachary's math test paper.

He'd gotten an A, Ryan noticed almost automatically, then stared at the statue once more. Priceless? And *here*? Obviously loved by the same woman who'd cried real tears as they'd buried a blue plastic cat clock?

Amazing.

"Well, you're not going to like *this*," Janna said as she breezed back into the room, her bathrobe nearly flying behind her as she plunked herself down beside him on the couch. "We're in for a siege, if the Internet is right. Five days, at the least—and that would be five *nights*, too, in case you're holding out for some good news. Only then can I get her...well, *fixed*. Oh, God, look, Ryan—she heard me. I can tell by the way she's glaring at me. Maybe we ought to *spell* from here on out?"

"Spell. In front of a cat." Ryan stabbed his fingers through his hair. "There's no other alternative?"

Janna leaned back on the couch and lifted one knee, grabbing hold of it with both hands as she began to rock. "Well, I guess we could spray her with Chanel, put a bow in her hair, teach her how to say 'Hell-ooo, sailor,' and throw her out the back door?"

Ryan got to his feet, partially because he was angry, but mostly because Janna needed neither Chanel nor bows nor snappy "lines" to have *his* full attention. "Very funny, Janna. You ought to take that act on the stage."

She stood up along with him. "Well, why not?

Help her out, that is? Zachary would just *adore* kittens.''

"I will *not* have a half-dozen kittens running around here,'' Ryan protested at once, mostly because he figured that was expected of him.

"And you won't,'' Janna pointed out, her hands on her hips, which he'd already learned wasn't exactly a good sign, not if he had hoped they'd get back on friendlier terms. ''I'll be back in my own house long before there'd be any kittens. I'd keep one, as company for T, and I'm sure I could find good homes for the others. Everyone in the neighborhood is crazy about T—she's such a great pal. Why, Pat—she lives next door—has already offered to buy Tansy from me, she's that crazy about her. T's a very *individual* cat, you know. Then I can get her F-I-X-E-D. So,'' she concluded, taking one hand from one hip—a good sign?—''know anybody who has a male cat?''

Tansy was rubbing up against his leg again, just as if she knew he could turn out to be her knight in shining armor. ''Five days and nights minimum, huh?'' he asked, looking down at the animal. ''Nobody should be adding to the pet population, so I've heard, but if you're planning to keep one kitten, and are sure you can find homes for the others…''

"Eeeooouuuwww! Yooowww! Eeeoowww!"

Ryan threw up his hands, admitting defeat. ''Oh, all right, all right! I'll call Jess in the morning. Her new next-door neighbor breeds cats.''

"Will that work?'' Janna asked, frowning. ''I mean, if the neighbor *breeds* cats, she's probably breeding Persians or something like that. Tansy's gorgeous, but she has no pedigree. I found her at the animal shelter. She may not want to have her cat breed with T.''

There was a part of Ryan's mind that was chanting: *I can't believe I'm even having this conversation.* ''Then I'll buy a damn male cat from her,'' he nearly exploded, as Tansy was at it again, yowling loud enough to wake the dead.

Well, close. Not the dead, but the door to the landing did open, and Allie came walking in, dressed in a flowing pink peignoir with pink-dyed feathers around her neck and tipping her matching slippers.

''Cat's in heat, huh?'' she said flatly, looking down at Tansy. ''Poor baby, I sympathize. Empathize, actually, at least from memory. Now, Mrs. Ballantine? Well, she'd probably get down on all fours on the floor and yowl along with you, because it has to have been twenty years since she—''

''Allie!'' Ryan all but screamed. He might be a grown man, but his grandmother still had the power to shock him. ''Behave yourself.''

Tansy, recognizing an ally—if not an ''Allie''— when she saw one, immediately began rubbing her length around Allie's ankles, purring loud enough to have anyone think she'd swallowed an outboard motor.

''There, there, baby,'' Allie said, leaning down to pat Tansy's head. Then she straightened, looked deeply into her grandson's eyes. ''Fix it, Ryan. Oh, don't look at me as if I just said you should eat fire or something. Not the cat, dear—fix the *situation*. Tomorrow. After all, if you don't mind seeing Mrs. Ballantine in her nightclothes, I'm sure I do, and she'll be up here sooner or later. Oh, and save a kitten for me, Janna. I didn't think I particularly liked cats, but they do sort of *grow* on you, don't they? Ryan, I'll be in your apartment, since the door is open. I'd like to speak to you when you're free."

"What about?" he asked, confused, his head sort of buzzing. "It's after midnight. Can't this wait until morning?"

"Probably, but I'll be leaving even earlier than you, to meet Charlie for breakfast, so we'll talk tonight. Unless that's a problem? I want to understand those papers you brought home from the office tonight, before I sign them."

"The papers? Oh, okay. No," Ryan said, sighing. He wasn't planning on sleeping tonight anyway. "No problem. I'll be with you in about fifteen minutes. Or sooner," he added, looking at Janna.

"Take your time, dear," Allie said, winking at Janna. "I'll just look around your bookshelves, possibly find something to read."

Janna lifted a hand no higher than her waist, and waggled her fingers at Allie. To Ryan's mind, the wave looked conspiratorial, but then he was tired and upset and probably wasn't thinking too clearly. Hell, he was still trying to figure out how he'd somehow agreed to pimp for a cat....

The next day, around noon, Ryan and Tansy and cat carrier pulled into Jessica's driveway. There were a few negotiations with the neighbor lady, he learned more than he needed to know about the intelligence and unique beauty of blue-cream domestic shorthaired cats, a sinfully large check was written, and he waved goodbye to Tansy, promising to pick her up again "um...*whenever.*"

He could have sworn the damn cat smiled at him before being taken away.

"I feel so dirty, so *used*," he quipped to Jessica as they retreated into the house for coffee; well, coffee for him, milk for Jessica.

She stopped in the doorway to turn and look at him. "Now *that's* funny, Ryan," she told him, kissing his cheek. "Maddy's right. You're like a whole new person since Janna and Zach moved in. I like the new you. I really, really do."

Ryan frowned, and tagged behind Jessica as they headed for the kitchen. "The new me? What was wrong with the old me?"

"The new you smiles more, I think, and frowns more, too. You're more *alive*." She leaned a hip against the kitchen counter and visually examined her brother. "You're not wearing a vest under that suit, your tie is loosened, and I even think your hair is longer. Did you forget to get a haircut, or does Janna like it better longer? And we won't even talk about the two of you playing basketball, will we? I think you looked twelve that night, Ryan. It was wonderful."

"You're reading an awful lot into a loosened tie and a forgotten barber appointment, Jess," he told her, motioning for her to take two glasses from the cabinet, so that he could have milk along with her.

"Really? Matt told me you canceled a meeting with his bank yesterday so you could go home early. We talked about it, and neither of us can remember when you've canceled a meeting—or gone home early. What was it? A pressing appointment with that adorable Zachary?"

Ryan bent his head, scratched at the side of his

neck. ''I promised to help him with his foul shot. He's decided to try out for one of the local youth teams. Don't read any more into it than that, Jess.''

''Uh-huh,'' Jessica said, walking past her brother, sliding her fingers along his cheek. ''You just keep fighting it, Ryan, the same way I did. You won't win, but keep on fighting. It makes the inevitable surrender so much the sweeter.''

Chapter Ten

Janna raised both hands—both empty, because she'd somehow lost her racket in that last, fruitless swing—and called out, "Uncle! Uncle! You win!"

Allie bounced the tennis ball she was holding, let it come up again, and deftly snagged it out of the air, putting it in her pocket. "Good thing, too. We were running out of balls," she said as she and Janna walked over to the bench, picked up towels to wipe their faces, slick with sweat even in this cool afternoon. "But, as I give Zach ten cents for each ball he finds in the bushes after you hit them there, I'm not worried."

"And Zach's getting rich," Janna said, grinning. "It's our plan, and it's working."

Allie looked at Janna for a moment, eyelids narrowed, then laughed. "You know, if anyone else said that, I'd just laugh. But with you? For all I know, you were on the pro circuit when you were Zachary's age. You've got depth, girl. Ryan will never be bored."

"You're still on that kick, huh? Hire the hall yet?" Janna asked, zipping her racket into its case.

"Not yet, but soon," Allie countered easily, handing Janna her own racket and bag. "Here, be a dear and take these up to the house, all right? I'll meet you there after I turn off the lights. I hate how we need them, sometimes even in the daytime, this time of year."

"Will there be broccoli included in the reception meal?" Janna persisted, zipping the racket into the bag, then following after Allie. "Like Jessica, Zachary hates broccoli. Maybe applesauce? He likes applesauce. And have you picked colors yet? Neon chartreuse for the bridesmaids is probably out."

"You're cute, Janna darling, but you can get on my nerves," Allie said, reaching inside a small metal box attached to a pole and switching off the overhead lights. "Why don't you just say it? Allie, butt out."

"Allie, butt out."

"Forget it," Allie countered swiftly, smiling. "I'm having way too much fun."

"Even after you looked at Ryan's bookshelves the other night?"

"*Especially* after I looked at Ryan's bookshelves the other night. I never knew, never even suspected, and I could flay myself alive for it. But *you* noticed. Not only did you notice, but he actually talked to you about it. Who would have thought he'd own at least two dozen books on education, child psychology, even a few teacher's handbooks? Not me, that's obvious. So trust me, darling, I'm not about to let you get away. Ryan needs you."

"So what you're saying, Allie, is that I don't have a choice."

"Something like that. You do love him, don't you?"

Janna bit her lips together, took a deep breath through her nose, blew it back out again. "I'm not going to answer that."

"Why? Because you don't? You don't know? Or because you love him so much it hurts? You can tell me."

"I'd rather have pins stuck in my eyes," Janna said, patting Allie on the shoulder. "If I love Ryan, Allie—and I'm not saying I do—then *he'll* be the first to hear it, okay?"

"And you'll help him? I could go to him, talk to him, but I know it wouldn't do any good. He's got this ridiculous sense of responsibility, and always has. He won't listen to me, he won't believe me. God knows he's never *confided* in me. Of the three of them, Ryan holds a special spot in my heart, just because he's so like his grandfather. Strong, independent, yet very vulnerable. And so *damn* stubborn."

Allie's thin shoulders sagged, and Janna impetuously hugged her, kissed her cheek. "You're such an old softie, Almira Chandler. I love *you*—does that count?"

Allie returned Janna's hug for a moment, then carefully disengaged herself—the smaller Allie being enthusiastically hugged by the tree-tall Janna was very much like being enveloped in the jaws of some benevolent, tie-dyed Venus's flytrap.

"Oh, look," she said, trying to hide her pleasure at Janna's spontaneous outpouring of affection, "I think that's Ryan, over on the driveway. It's only four o'clock, whatever can he be doing home so early again? I've seen him work until eight o'clock on

Christmas Eve, but I haven't had a call telling me
he'd be late for dinner ever since you and Zachary
moved in. And you can think what you like about
that, my dear, but I already have come to my own
conclusions.''

"Yes, but you haven't yet rented the hall?" Janna
reconfirmed.

"No. I'm too afraid you'll want to be married bare-
foot in some meadow, with daisies in your hair and
poor Ryan in a pastel-blue tuxedo with pink ruffled
shirt. You won't, will you?''

Janna laughed, and hugged her again, and Allie
started liking those hugs more and more.

He'd had some crazy ideas in his time, Ryan knew,
but this one definitely was on the way to taking first
prize for Dumb. Whatever had possessed him to believe he could fix a bike chain?

A rational man would have bought the kid a bike
if he wanted the kid to have a bike. That was what a
rational man would have done.

But Janna had said that doing the work himself—
like putting the basketball hoop together—made the
gift mean that much more, to everyone. She might
have been right about the hoop; he still kind of smiled
each time he saw it, remembered the three of them
pretending to be raising the flag on Iwo Jima as they'd
finally gotten it together and then lifted the completed
hoop upright.

But dragging your old bike out of the loft above
the garages and trying to reattach the chain, when you
already know you have the mechanical skills of a
cross-eyed amoeba?

That was just plain nuts.

He also hadn't known that bicycle grease had a half-life much like that of radioactive waste, that it could still be present in such quantity twenty-some years after the last time he'd ridden the bike. He'd since learned that not only was the grease still hanging around, it transferred easily to skin. And cloth. And hair.

He looked down at his hands, shook his head, and decided to go use the utility washtub in the garages to wash off, start over. He thought this because he was, at heart, a very neat man, and because if he had to look at that damned chain another moment, he might just bite it.

Pressing in the code that opened the last of the three garage doors, he waited for it to raise, then stepped inside…and stopped dead. The garage wall was in bloom.

From front to back, the wall holding the utility sink was covered in at least eight-foot-high sunflowers painted right on the previously beige-painted cinder block.

Huge sunflowers. Tall green stalks, deep green leaves, and heavy, bending sunflower heads with bright yellow petals.

It was a forest of sunflowers.

"What the—"

"Like it?" Janna asked from behind him, and he turned to see her standing there, her hands behind her back, rocking on her heels. And smiling at him. "Makes the place cheerier, doesn't it?"

Ryan raised a hand to rub at his forehead, then thought better of it when he saw the grease on that hand. Under his fingernails. Grease. Grease everywhere. And sunflowers.

"Do I *like* it?" he asked, heading for the utility sink which, he noticed, had also been decorated with sunflowers, these in miniature, and in a pink painted vase on the front of the sink. "Do I *like* it? Let me tell you something, Janna…." He closed his mouth, opened it again, then gave a silent chuckle, amazed at himself. "Yeah. Yeah, I like it a lot, actually."

Janna relaxed her breath in a long sigh. "Oh, good. I was so worried you might not. Like the flowers, that is. And I did ask Allie first if I could do it."

"And she said…?" Ryan asked, soaping his hands.

"She *said* I could paint anything I wanted on the wall, except for nasty words or phrases like *for a good time, call*…" Janna handed Ryan a fistful of paper towels from the dispenser next to the sink. "I just love it when Allie tries to be hip, don't you?"

"Tries? Janna, Allie *invented* hip." Ryan tossed the used towels in the trash can, then stepped back and admired the wall once more. Now he saw a few butterflies flitting across the wall, perched on flower heads; and some of those flower heads were sporting happy faces smiles. There was even a bluebird sitting on one of the huge leaves. It was…well, it was a *happy* picture, and so very like Janna. "It does sort of bring the outside in, doesn't it? Is this it, or are you planning on painting all the walls? Oh, and did you sign this one? I think I'd like it even better if you'd sign and date it."

Janna took his arm and led him toward the front of the garage, then pointed to the seeming smudge near the floor line that, on closer inspection, turned out to be Janna's name and the date. "Now you can tell everyone you have an authentic Monroe. It makes things more valuable, to have them signed and dated.

Why, in five hundred years, this wall could be worth at least ten dollars.''

Her words put Ryan in mind of the figurine he'd seen on the coffee table last night. "You mean, like that naked lady figurine you have upstairs?" he asked.

"Oh, you mean Ethel," Janna said, smiling. "Do you like her?"

"That depends," he said, keying in the code so that the door slid back down along its track. "Is that the real thing up there? The same one shown on the cover of your parents' book?"

Janna was approaching the bike, looking at it as it lay on its side, the chain guard off, exposing the bike's current problem. "Oh, sure, Ethel's for real."

Ryan swallowed, remembering the ponytail band draped over one of the figurine's arms. "Real," he repeated. "In the book, the figurine is said to be priceless."

Janna went down on her knees beside the bike, and turned her head to smile up at him. "And you believe that poppycock?"

"*Poppycock?* People still use that word? And, yes, why shouldn't I believe it?"

She sat back on her heels, breathed a sigh. "Ethel is priceless, Ryan, because Sam never put a price on her. He and Mary found it on a dig they'd financed themselves, so he kept it, but he never officially priced it. *Priceless.* Understand now?"

"So how much is it worth?" he asked, picking up a screwdriver and trying to wedge it under the chain so he could pull the thing back onto the gear teeth.

"Oh, it couldn't be more than ten, twenty."

The chain, nearly in place, popped off yet again. *"Thousand?"*

"Here, give me that," Janna said, taking the screwdriver from him, then deftly popping the chain back onto the gears. "Yes, thousand. But that's not the point."

"It's not?" He looked around a little, tried to remember he was still in Allentown, he hadn't fallen down some rabbit hole again. "Then what is the point?"

"The *point,* Ryan," Janna told him as he helped her right the bike, "is that I was six years old, ready to go off to school, and this was my last dig except for summers. I liked Ethel, and Sam gave her to me for my birthday. *That's* what makes it priceless. Understand now?"

"Not in a million years," Ryan said, but he wasn't quite telling the truth. He did understand, or thought he was at least beginning to understand. Things, to Janna, were just things, just as she said. They could be worth pennies, or thousands of dollars. That didn't matter to her. But memories, well, memories were forever. "You could give that figurine to a museum tomorrow and not miss it, couldn't you?"

"Oh, I'd miss it, Ryan. And I won't give it away because I don't have to, and Ethel can't walk away on her own, or burn down, or…or die. But, yes, the memory of Ethel would be just as dear to me as Ethel herself, if that's what you mean."

"I don't know *what* I mean," Ryan told her honestly. "Didn't you ever think about selling the—selling Ethel, when money got tight after Mark died?"

"Who said money got tight?" Janna countered, frowning down at the two flat bike tires. "I just said

I had to work to support Zachary and myself. There's a difference.''

"Sure. Sure there is. What's the difference?''

Janna walked the bike over to the garage door and propped it there, then turned to look at Ryan. "You really want to get into this?" she asked.

"Yeah, I really do,'' Ryan answered honestly. "Because right now I'm confused as all hell. We can talk while we take the bike to the gas station to blow up those tires.''

"All right," Janna said warily, and waited for him to load the bike into the back of his SUV, then pull the seldom-used vehicle out of the center garage. She climbed into the front passenger seat and buckled herself in, then looked at Ryan's profile as he checked the rearview mirror as he backed out of the driveway.

"It's like this, Ryan," she said once they'd blended into the light traffic on the highway a few blocks from the house. "Mark and I lived on what he made on his art, the little I made on mine, because that's how we wanted it. After Mark died, I started my own business and Zachary and I lived—live—on that. Ethel, and my trust fund, that sort of thing, well, they'd be too easy. Besides, I want to save all of that for Zachary.''

"Okay, now that last one makes sense, saving everything for Zachary. But the rest of it, Janna? You gave up your art, remember?''

"That was my choice, Ryan. I'm not really all that good, you know. Maybe I was even happy to give it up, so that I didn't have to let the world know how not very good I am.''

"But you *are* good.''

"I'm adequate. Competent. And I enjoy what I do.

I just don't have any burning desire to see my work hanging in the Metropolitan. I paint, create, when I want to, when I feel like creating, and that's enough. I'd be just as happy painting scenery for a local theater group as I would be lying on my back and doing another Sistine Chapel. Mark never quite understood that. Do you?''

Ryan stopped at a red light and turned to look at Janna. "Yes," he said slowly, "yes, I think I do. And, if you'll excuse my being cynical here, you always know you have enough money behind you if you want to scrap the web page design business and paint full-time, right?''

Janna tipped her head to one side, frowned, then allowed a slow smile to light her face. "I never thought about it that way but, yes, I suppose that's always in the back of my head." She sat up very straight in her bucket seat. "Isn't that *wonderful!* I'm doing what I want, because I want to do it, but I could do another thing I wanted, if I wanted to do it. Just like you—except I don't think you want to do what you're doing. You just won't do what you want because you don't want it *enough.* Like I don't want my art enough.''

Ryan felt his spine stiffening. "How did we get back to me? I thought the subject of my teaching was just about exhausted?''

"Well, it shouldn't have been, should it? Because now I understand. Your teaching, my art. Neither of us wants it enough." She shook her head, causing her mushroom-cloud curls to wiggle about on the top of her head. "No, that's not exactly right. Because I'm happy. You're not, and you've said as much yourself.''

Ryan pulled into the gas station and parked the car beside the air pump, slamming the gearshift into Park. "I never said I wasn't happy, damn it," he said, wondering why he'd thought having another conversation with Janna would get him anywhere. The only thing that would *get* him anywhere would be to hit the lever that put the seat back and lay her down, kiss her until they were both senseless, couldn't think at all.

Janna rolled her eyes comically. "Oh, brother, here we go. Methinks he doth protest too much, ladies and gentlemen. You are *so* not happy, Ryan. Allie sees it, a blind man could—"

"*Allie* sees it?" Ryan interrupted, taking hold of one of Janna's lightly fluttering hands. "*That's* why she signed me up for that damn auction, then sicced you on me? Because she knows I'm not happy? Not just that she wanted me to have a little fun, shake me up a little, like she said? She thinks I'm *unhappy*? What's next, Janna—she fixes me up on a blind date with a psychiatrist?"

"Oh, for pity's sake, calm down," Janna said, prying his fingers from her wrist. "Allie's your grandmother and she loves you, and she knows you're not happy. And if you tell me one more time that you are too happy, I may have to hurt you, Ryan Chandler!"

Ryan looked at Janna, who was rubbing her wrist, then looked down at his hands, now closed into fists. He opened them slowly, tried to regain control over his usually placid but now boiling-hot temper. "Did you tell her?" he asked quietly, rubbing at his forehead. "Did you report in after every conversation we've had, keep Allie up to date? Does she *know*?"

Janna coughed into her fist, turned to look out the

window in the vain hope someone, anyone, would
come to her rescue. "She might have guessed...."

"She might have guessed. Oh, that's beautiful, that
is. She might have *guessed.* So now Allie thinks she
knows why I'm not happy, and that I'd *be* happy if I
could just walk away from the family business, go
back to school, get my teaching degree. Is that it?"

"Actually," Janna said, turning to look at him once
more, "right now, Allie's still pretty set on getting
the two of us together. I'm not sure she really believes
you're unhappy because of your job, your responsibilities to the family. Do they really need you *that*
much, Ryan? I mean, aren't you maybe putting too
much importance on who runs the business?"

Ryan put his hand on the door handle. "Oh, good,
good. Now you're going to tell me I've got a big
head, that I can't believe the family business could
go on without me. Well, thanks a lot, Janna."

"You're welcome. So, can it go on without you?"
Janna asked, grabbing Ryan's forearm, keeping him
from getting out of the car. "Can you go on without
it? Is it safer there, in your office, than it would be if
you chased your dream? Is that it, Ryan? Are you
afraid to take a chance?"

Ryan looked down at Janna's hand for a long moment, then shook it off, got out of the car, pulled the
bike from the rear compartment.

Neither of them spoke all the way back to the
house.

Chapter Eleven

"You and Mom have a fight?"

Ryan caught the basketball on the rebound, and held it. He turned to look at Zachary, who was looking at him a little too intensely for comfort.

He hadn't heard the boy's approach, probably because he was concentrating on various snappy replies he could have made to Janna yesterday at the gas station. That, and he was kind of distracted by the fact that he'd also been mentally kicking himself around the driveway for the past hour.

How had he survived all these years without this basketball hoop? He didn't need therapy. He just needed a better jump shot.

"What makes you think we had a fight, Zach?" he asked, tucking the basketball under his arm, then using his free hand to motion the boy out onto the driveway, toward the foul line and keyhole Janna had painted on the macadam. "Want to play a little one-on-one?"

"Sure," Zachary said, brushing his red hair back off his forehead and putting out his hands to take the ball. "And you're sure you didn't have a fight?" he asked, starting to dribble. "Mom usually doesn't draw pictures of people and then yell at them. At least, not much anyway. She can be kinda, you know, *strange?*"

Ryan stopped dead, trying to envision Janna yelling at a drawing of himself, and Zachary breezed past him for an easy layup. "She yelled at a drawing of me? How do you know it was of me?"

Zachary threw him the basketball. "Well, it was pretty easy, because she had your head *real* big, and your body was little, but all in a suit, and you were carrying a briefcase that said Big Stupid Businessman on it."

"Oh," Ryan said, beginning to move with the ball, "I guess you're right. It had to be me. Did you overhear what she was yelling, er, saying to the drawing?"

"She called you names," Zachary said, easily stealing the ball, just as easily sinking a two-handed jump shot just the way Ryan had taught him. "She can make up some really nifty names, too. One time she called me a folly-fallen plume-plucked miscreant. She says it's fractured Shakespeare. She found a whole list on the Internet one day. Cool, huh?"

"Frigid," Ryan said, drawing on his years-old supply of teen slang. "Did she call me anything like that?"

"Oh, yeah. But lots worse. She even mumbled some of it, which means it wasn't something for little pitchers with big ears, like Mrs. Ballantine says almost every time I come into the kitchen when she and Allie are talking. You want to keep playing, or what?''

"To tell you the truth, Zach, I think I'd rather go find your mother, and see that picture. Do you mind staying out here a while, while I talk to her?''

"Nope. I kind of like to find something else to do when Mom's mad, because that's always when she decides I ought to clean my room or something.''

"I can see where you're coming from, Zach," Ryan said, ruffling the boy's hair. "I won't tell her where you are, okay?''

"Okay. Be careful," he called after Ryan, "or she'll have you cleaning something, too.''

Ryan crossed the backyard lawn, making for the white wooden staircase that curved up to the second floor, to a railed porch atop the jut-out of the downstairs sunroom, then continued inside the house, all the way up to the landing between the two third-floor apartments.

The stairs had been one of his grandfather's ideas, so that swimmers could get straight to the bedroom areas without tramping through the main floor of the house. Of course, his grandfather hadn't thought far enough ahead to realize that three inventive teens considered that staircase a great way to escape the house at night.

Which explained the dead bolt on the door, and the fact that Allie had ordered it installed and had kept the only key until Maddy went off to college.

Why Ryan thought about this now, and smiled at the memory, told him that he was grasping at straws, trying to think of anything that didn't have to do with finding Janna and seeing the disappointment in her big brown eyes.

Because she was disappointed in him; that much was clear. It was part of the reason he was angry with her, because he'd made it a lifelong mission never to disappoint anyone. But it wasn't the main reason.

The main reason he didn't want to see Janna was because she was right. He *was* a Big Stupid Businessman. And not much more, unfortunately.

He was just reaching for the doorknob leading indoors when Jessica opened the door and stepped out onto the porch. "Hi, Ryan. I was just upstairs, dropping off Tansy. Mission accomplished, according to Maryjane, my neighbor."

"How is she?"

Jessica shrugged her shoulders. "She didn't say," she then said, smiling at him. "But she isn't yelling anymore, so that's probably a good sign, right?"

"Yelling?" Ryan shook his head. "Zach said— you actually *heard* her yelling?"

Jessica cocked her head to one side, looked at Ryan curiously. "Brother of mine, I'm talking about Tansy. Who are you talking about?"

Spreading his hands in front of him as if to ward off Jessica's last question until he could gather his wits about him, Ryan said, "Tansy, of course. I was talking about Tansy. She, um, she was screeching up a storm last time I saw her."

"Well, she's not now," Jessica reported, still looking at Ryan as if she knew he was hiding something, she didn't know quite what, but she'd be damned if she'd leave this spot until she found out. "Oh, wait, I've got it. You and Janna—you've been fighting, haven't you? Now, why would you go and do a stupid thing like that? Janna's a terrific person."

"A little nuts, but a terrific person," Ryan concluded for her.

"Okay, yes, a little nuts—but a wonderful sort of nuts. Do you know what we did upstairs just now? She got a length of thread and a needle, suspended the needle over my belly, and then we watched as the needle started to move."

Ryan pinched the bridge of his nose between thumb and forefinger. "I should have eaten lunch. I think I'm light-headed."

"No, no, seriously, Ryan," Jessica said. "She threaded the needle—doubled the thread—then suspended the needle over the babies. She told me the needle would go back and forth for a boy, and move in a circle if it was a girl. At least I think that was it—maybe it was the other way around? Anyway, the needle actually began to move. Janna stopped it, and it began to move again. All by itself! And it was right—both times. Can you believe that?"

"I once believed in Santa Claus and the Easter Bunny, so I guess I could believe in a thread-and-needle sex test—until I was, oh, about eight years old. Jessica, you don't really believe Janna could predict the sex of your kids like that, do you?"

"She did it, Ryan," Jessica reminded him. "I already knew the sex, didn't I? The thread and needle just confirmed what the ultrasound already showed. Oh, and according to Janna, I'm going to have two more children before Matt and I think our family is complete. I know their sex now, too. We're going to end up with two boys and two girls, although I'm not going to tell you which ones will be which. Isn't that wonderful?"

Ryan looked at his smart, levelheaded, practical

sister for long moments. "Who *are* you?" he asked at last. "And what did you do with the *real* Jessica?"

Jessica stood on tiptoe and kissed Ryan's cheek. "I love you when you're baffled, brother dear," she said, then stepped past him, on her way toward the stairs. "Oh, and if you and Janna *are* fighting? Apologize, dear. Because I'm sure, whatever it is, you're wrong. Bye!"

And so, forewarned by Zachary, and pretty much told he was an idiot by a fat-bellied sister who'd placed her utter confidence in a needle and thread, Ryan entered the house, headed up the stairs to Maddy's apartment.

Men had been known to walk with more of a spring to their step on the way to the gallows.

"I know, Jack, I know. Stoves don't just pop out of the sky, just like you said." Janna held the phone away from her ear for a moment, looking at it owlishly, then put it against her ear once more. "Where *do* they pop out of, Jack?"

She listened for a few moments, as Jack—her contractor—explained warehouse backlog and shipping schedules, her mind pretty much on stun. Finally, she interrupted. "Jack—Jack! How about I just come on over to the house, look at that book of yours again and pick out another stove? Would that help?"

Jack was silent for a few moments—a blessing in any case, to Janna's mind—and then agreed. He then went on to give her more updates on the refrigerator, the cabinets, the countertop. Except for the missing stove, Jack felt certain the kitchen would be usable in the next two days. The upstairs wasn't complete, and none of the final painting could be done for another week but, yes, she could conceivably move back in by the weekend.

"Thanks, Jack, that's all I needed to hear. You're a sweetheart. Remind me to give you a big kiss when I come to pick out the new stove. Oh? You won't be there? Well, there's a pity. Bye now!"

She hung up the phone and leaned back against the counter in the galley kitchen. It was a lovely kitchen, but it wasn't *her* kitchen, and it was time she was back in her own house.

Away from Ryan. Away from the whole Chandler family whom she was beginning to care for more than was probably practical.

By the weekend, Jack had said. That left only four days between now and Move Out time. She had that project to complete for Givens Electronics, with no other deadlines for another two weeks, so she could finish up the Givens, then spend at least a week getting acquainted with her new kitchen, painting the walls herself. Jack hadn't liked hearing that, and didn't understand why she felt the need to do the work herself, the need she had to put her own stamp back on a house that had been home for several years but now felt like a part of her past, not her future.

Which was stupid. It was, after all, *her* house. She and Zachary had come to Allentown, made that small Cape Cod house their own. They'd painted the mural, decorated the kitchen, painted the ceiling of Zach's room to resemble the solar system.

It was *their* house.

Why did she feel now, in the deepest parts of her, that it would no longer be their *home?*

The fire had only changed the physical structure a little, and not permanently. If she wanted, she could recreate the kitchen and her bedroom and bath, make them look the same, as if the fire had never happened.

Except she didn't want to do that. She didn't know why; she just didn't.

She also couldn't really become enthusiastic about redecorating, taking the spaces and redoing them, re-forming them.

She had thought she and Zachary were complete. Just the two of them; a small family, definitely missing Mark, but complete by themselves. The house had "fit" that picture of herself, of Zachary.

Now it didn't fit. Nothing fit.

"Ryan," she grumbled under her breath, because she might believe her feelings were stupid, but she wasn't stupid enough not to know why she felt the way she felt.

It was his fault, all of it.

She'd only seen Mark with Zachary when their son was a baby. He'd been a good daddy, a loving daddy. But Mark hadn't lived to stand behind Zach, his larger hands over Zachary's smaller ones, helping him line up a foul shot. Mark hadn't lived to listen to Zachary's "boys only" secrets, or to teach him how to ride a two-wheeler, or so many other father-son things she had believed she could handle on her own without Zachary feeling the lack.

But these days Zachary's every other sentence began with, "Ryan says..." Janna knew that a line had been crossed in Zachary's life, a line he'd perhaps imagined but never spoken of—the line between what is "done" by a mom and what is "done" with a dad.

Zachary would survive, be all right, once they were back in their little house and Ryan was gone. He'd survive, but he'd feel the lack. That was a pity.

But it wasn't the worst of it, not by a long shot.

Zachary didn't just like Ryan, didn't just enjoy his company while they were doing "boy things." He genuinely loved Ryan, which was clear as Janna sat with him as he said his evening prayers and Zachary thanked God for Ryan being in his life.

Janna winced inwardly. That had hurt, hearing Zachary thank God for Ryan. She didn't say anything to the boy, certainly didn't have to remind Zachary not to forget to say a prayer for his daddy in heaven before she tucked him into bed. But it still hurt.

It hurt because Ryan was not going to have a place in Zachary's life, or in hers.

Janna sighed, looked around the kitchen, then down at Tansy, who was rubbing up against her leg. "Sure," she said, "*you're* happy. You don't even begin to understand the word *consequences,* do you? Oh, no. You're just one big party animal. You take what you want when you want it, and you'll worry about the consequences later. I can't do that, T, although I wish I could. Just wait until you have kids, T, *then* you'll understand."

Ryan heard Janna's voice as he walked into the apartment's living room. He'd knocked, and the door had opened because Jessica must not have closed it properly when she left.

"Probably too much in a hurry to go home and tell poor Matt they're going to have four kids, not just these two, Lord help him," Ryan said, shaking his head. Then, not able to help himself, he smiled. Jessica was so happy, and his sister deserved to be happy. Maddy deserved to be happy.

So why didn't he think *he* did? Isn't that what

Janna had asked, or at least alluded to? Why *didn't* he think he deserved to be happy, follow his dream?

Was it some overblown sense of responsibility?

Or was Janna right, and he was just plain scared?

"Janna?" he called out, wanting to make sure of his welcome before he poked his head into the kitchen and possibly got beaned by a frying pan. He didn't actually believe Janna would ever resort to physical violence, but she was just unpredictable enough for it to be a possibility.

Which was one of the many things he loved about her, adored about her...would miss so much when she was gone.

Gone? What made him think she'd be gone? Sure, she'd be moving back into her house soon, that was a given. But gone? Why did she have to be gone?

"Because she thinks you're an idiot, and probably a bad influence on her son, that's why," he said, answering himself out loud, then stopping dead as his own words shamed him.

Then angered him.

Who the hell was Janna Monroe to call him a coward? Huh? *Who?* She hadn't lived his life. She hadn't grown up watching an irresponsible father run as far and as fast as he could from the family business that paid for his jet-setting life while robbing years from his own father's life, Ryan's beloved grandfather's life.

Somebody had to be responsible, act responsibly. Not for the money, because the company was well-established, and could either be sold for a comfortable fortune or put into the hands of managers. It was because it was *family*. Ryan saw that. Janna obviously couldn't.

And why should she? She'd been shuttled around all of her growing-up years, if he could assume that from the little she'd told him. Her parents had been self-sufficient, more than self-sufficient—perhaps even selfish—and Janna hadn't felt necessary to them, even irreplaceable.

She'd grown up obviously independent, a little outrageous, and telling herself that people leaving her, even Mark's death, was all right, because she was self-sufficient, had her memories.

Yet she'd cried over that stupid blue cat clock. Cried real tears over a thing, a replaceable thing. She'd recovered quickly, but she'd been shaken. And hated that he'd seen her shaken.

The mural had been damaged beyond repair? That's okay, she'd paint another one, if she wanted to. The kitchen had been gutted? That was okay, too, and she was looking forward to building new memories.

Always the optimist, always looking ahead, looking at life as a glass at least half-full. Her husband's death had to have been devastating, and Ryan knew she had loved Mark with all the considerable emotion she was capable of...but she had somehow survived that loss, even rationalized it in her mind.

As if a person could ever rationalize the death of a loved one. Janna hadn't just decided to leave New York after Mark died. She'd run away. She was probably getting ready to run away yet again.

Ryan wasn't about to let her go.

"Janna!" he repeated, louder this time, walking toward the kitchen. "Where are you? We have to talk!"

Chapter Twelve

In the midst of spooning Irish-Cream-flavored coffee beans into the grinder she'd brought from her house, Janna stopped dead, the spoon suspended in the air, and made a terrible face. "Ryan," she muttered, narrowing her eyes, looking around the kitchen and knowing there was no way out of the room without passing through the living room. "Busted!"

She finished measuring out beans as she put a smile on her face and called out that she was in the kitchen, and why didn't he join her for a cup of coffee. Then she took a deep breath, willed her smile to be more natural, and turned to watch him enter the room.

Oh, yeah, she was busted, all right. And she knew who to blame: Zachary. He'd seen the caricature, heard her talking to it, and had gone straight to Ryan to tell him. Men were like that: they stuck together, no matter what.

The caricature! Janna looked about wildly, hoping

to see it. No, no, it wasn't there. Where had she left it?

"Looking for this?" Ryan asked from the doorway. She whirled around to see him leaning one shoulder against the doorjamb, his long legs crossed at the ankles, his dark hair tousled, and with the caricature waving in front of him—definitely not as a flag of truce.

Janna wiped a finger under the tip of her nose and struck her best "I'm a bad gangster" pose. "The kid squealed, did he? What did you use, thumbscrews? Brass knuckles? Or did he just turn stoolie on his own?"

Ryan rolled up the sheet of paper, handed it to her. "I saw it on the coffee table," he said. "The resemblance is pretty clear, although I think I'd like to take issue on my ears. They definitely don't stick out that much."

"Artistic license," Janna said, searching in a drawer for a rubber band, then slipping it over the rolled-up paper. "Besides, it would be way too obvious to give you a Pinocchio nose."

"For lying?" Ryan looked at her closely, felt her nervousness. "Who did I lie to?"

"Yourself, for starters," Janna said, wishing the coffee would perk faster, so she'd have something to do with her hands. "Your grandmother, your sisters…and anybody else who believes you enjoy being head of the family business, burying your dreams and your talents, wasting them both."

"Second verse, same as the first, huh?" Ryan said, shaking his head. "It must be nice, being so perfect, being able to see everyone else's imperfections, failings, shortcomings."

"I'm not perfect," Janna said, reaching in the cupboard for two coffee mugs. "Far from it. I run away, too, Ryan. But I run—I ran—from what *was,* not from what could be. There's a difference."

Ryan opened his mouth to protest, then closed it again. "You're right," he said at last. "There is a difference. And you'll be running again, won't you? I don't know why I feel that, but I do. And this time you'll be running from me."

"Not running, Ryan," Janna said carefully. "Backing away, backing off. Not taking another step forward, much as I want to, because I'd only add to your unhappiness."

Ryan brought his closed fist down on the countertop, amazing himself with his vehemence. "I'm *not* that damn unhappy, damn it!"

That verbal explosion wasn't quite articulate, and he knew it, but he also knew he meant what he had said—okay, yelled. He *wasn't* that damn unhappy.

"I'm not, Janna," he repeated, striving to control himself, control this new emotion welling up inside him, asking to be recognized. "I'm not that unhappy. I've got a loving family, great friends, a successful business. I've got my books and, yes, even my dreams. Just because I don't act on those dreams doesn't mean I can't enjoy them, either."

"If you say so," Janna said, turning away to pick up the coffeepot, then pouring them each a cup of the fragrant brew. "It is your choice, isn't it?"

"Yes. Yes, it is. Just as it was your choice to put away your art because you were afraid—yes, Janna, *afraid*—you weren't good enough. No wonder you get so bent out of shape about me. I'm *you,* aren't I? Take away the three-piece suit and the tie-dyed

T-shirts, and we're pretty much the same. We just give what we are different titles. You're the carefree flower child with family responsibilities, and I'm the overworked businessman with family responsibilities. There's no difference, Janna. You're *me*. You have the trust fund, the *money*, the financial freedom, to follow your dream. But you won't, you can't. You're too afraid you're not good enough. And that's why you can't stand to see me do what you're doing…and not doing what you're afraid to do. God! Why didn't I see this before?''

"Go away, Ryan," Janna said, pouring his cup of coffee into the sink. "Just go away, live your life, and let Zachary and me alone."

He stepped behind her, put his hands on her shoulders, turned her around. "Not on your life, Janna," he breathed into her ear.

His words weakened her, his warm breath melted her resistance, so that she had no choice but to lay her head against him, supported by his strength. "Please, Ryan, just go. Don't believe in me this way. Mark did, and it was too great a burden. Why can't I just keep painting sunflowers?"

"You can," Ryan said, "if you want to live your whole life wondering…wondering if maybe you were wrong and Mark was right. Just like you've forced me to wonder if I'll spend the rest of my life wondering if you're right about me, and I'm wrong. We're a pair of pathetic messes, aren't we?"

Janna reached up, traced a finger down Ryan's cheek. "I don't know what to say…."

Ryan smiled. "Neither do I," he admitted honestly. "But I do know I don't want you to run, Janna. I don't want you out of my life."

He kissed her then, softly, sweetly, and she wrapped her arms around his neck, drawing him closer to her, fitting herself against him...and she fit perfectly.

"Are you and Janna getting along?" Allie asked as Ryan propped the morning paper against the juice pitcher and began spooning grapefruit into his mouth. "I could baby-sit, I suppose, if you two want to go off by yourselves for a few days, have some long...talks?"

The wedge of grapefruit stuck somewhere partway down Ryan's throat, and he coughed and finally had to wipe his eyes with his linen napkin before glaring down the table at his grandmother. "Aren't you late for your meeting with the witch's coven?" he asked as Allie sat at the foot of the table, her face a mask of innocence.

"Don't sass your grandmother," Mrs. Ballantine said, leaning over his shoulder to grab up the newspaper. "And don't read at the table. It's impolite."

Ryan looked up at the housekeeper, resplendent in her usual funereal black dress and bright-red lipstick. "Oh? Reading the paper is wrong, but Allie asking me if I want her to baby-sit so I can go somewhere and shack up with Janna is all right? No wonder you two get along so well. You're both nuts."

"We're both reasonable adults," Mrs. Ballantine said. "Or do you think no one has noticed the way you and Miss Monroe are all but drooling on each other these past few days?"

"Go get 'em, Lucille!" Allie called down the table encouragingly. "We're living vicariously now, Ryan darling, but that doesn't mean we think you should be parading your *longings* in front of Zachary. Unless you're seriously considering marrying Janna, in which case, well, have at it, darling, with our blessings.''

Ryan went on the alert. "Zachary? How does Zach fit into all of this? Have you been talking to him?''

Allie patted her lips with her napkin, then carefully placed it on the table. "No, darling, I have not. But Zachary has been talking to me. And he's asked me if I'd really want to live in this big house all alone. Now, why do you think he asked me that? He was quite concerned, by the way, and promised he'd always be able to come visit, swim in the pool, play basketball, and have lunch with me if Lucille here promises to keep cutting the crusts off his bologna sandwiches. I thought that was very generous of him, don't you? Although I'm still not quite sure if Zachary sees the three of you in your own home, or if he just wants to move into this one.''

Ryan sighed, scratched at a spot behind his ear. "Oh, brother.''

"My sentiments exactly. Poor child, of course we want him and his mother here. Lord knows there's room enough for an army, so don't go thinking about taking them away from us, you hear me?'' Mrs. Ballantine said, then swept out the room, taking the morning newspaper with her.

"Don't be angry with Lucille, darling. Zachary has her wrapped right around his little finger, in case you haven't noticed.'' Allie walked down the length of the table and sat in the chair nearest Ryan's. "Darling, I know I've been endlessly wonderful throughout all of this, minding my own business—''

"God, I love the way your mind works,'' Ryan

interrupted, chuckling wryly. "You'd probably even pass a lie detector test. But, please, go on."

"But," Allie continued, "I'm worried about Zachary now. Yes, you and Janna seem to be getting on much better these days, but I'm not seeing what I want to see, or hearing what I want to hear. There are still problems, aren't there? And, if you can't work them out, I'm afraid Zachary is going to be hurt. He adores you, you know."

"And I'm crazy about him," Ryan said, scratching at that same spot behind his ear once more. "Janna and I—well, yes, maybe we do have some problems."

"Ya think?" Allie snapped, showing an amazing affinity for the latest in sarcastic, short-speak slang. "It's not the boots, is it? Because I'm rather getting used to those."

Ryan looked at his grandmother, getting the sinking feeling that the woman was trying much too hard to play this scene "light," not saying what was really on her mind. This was so unusual that he found it hard to believe, but he thought he'd test her, see just how much she knew.

"Janna is afraid to seriously pursue her art, her painting," he said, then sat back and watched, waited.

"Well, yes, of course you're afraid, Ryan darling," Allie responded quickly, "but if you really want— *What did you say?"*

"Oh, no," Ryan said, pushing back his chair and standing up. "Not what did I say, but what did you just say? You were trying to set me up, weren't you, Allie? And you were so sure where you were leading me you only half listened to my answer before beginning what I'm sure would have been a really great,

well-rehearsed monologue. Stop me when I'm wrong,
okay?''

"Busted," Allie said under her breath, sounding
very much like Janna. She lifted her head, smiled up
at her grandson. "You weren't going to tell me that
Janna is disappointed in you because you want to
teach but won't do anything about it, were you?''

"Nope," Ryan returned, just about popping the
word out of his pursed mouth. He had to keep his lips
pursed; otherwise he'd be laughing out loud. "Not
even close.''

"I *told* you," Mrs. Ballantine said, placing a fresh
cup of tea in front of Allie. "You're getting too old
for this, no matter how many nips and tucks you've
got that make you think you're still as young as you
used to be. The boy just did a fine dance around you,
and now you're stuck. Serves you right.''

"You're fired," Allie said, picking up her teacup,
knowing Lucille Ballantine had already sweetened it
for her.

"Oh, goodie, again? That's only the second time
this week," Mrs. Ballantine said, then sailed out of
the room once more, like a battleship in full sail...if
the sails could be black. Maybe she was a pirate ship?

And why am I thinking about Mrs. Ballantine and
ships, Ryan thought, before he sat down again to look
at his grandmother. "I love you, you know," he said,
reaching over to pat her hand. "You're a pain in
the...pain in the neck, but I do love you.''

"But I'm *old*," Allie said, and Ryan was surprised
to hear the defeat in his grandmother's voice. But
then, why should he be surprised? Everyone had their
own secrets, their own dreams, and definitely their
own fears. Allie's was, always had been, that of grow-

ing old, and infirm, and—knowing Allie—a *burden*
to her grandchildren.

"Old, young, fat, skinny, nipped and tucked or
sagged and bagged, I love you, Almira Chandler. We
all do," Ryan said, squeezing her hand, holding it
between both of his. "Okay?"

If nothing else could be said about Almira Chandler, she was not the sort to whine or pine or indulge
in long self-pity parties.

To prove this, she looked at her grandson, maybe
seeing her own husband lurking somewhere in his
green eyes, and said brightly, "So you'll sell the business and go back to school, become a teacher? Marry
Janna, move the two of them in here, and live happily
ever after?"

"Become a teacher." Ryan let go of Allie's hand,
used both of his to cover his face as he moaned low
in his throat. "What did she do, Allie, rent a bill-
board? Who else knows about this?"

"Nobody," Allie said quickly. Too quickly, so that
Ryan let his hands fall away from his face and looked
at her piercingly. "Oh, all right. Lucille, she knows
everything, always has. And Joe—he was particularly
interested, considering the fact that I think he buys a
new business every week. And Matt, of course, as
he's our banker."

"Joe and Matt," Ryan repeated. "That would
mean Maddy and Jess know, too. You do know that
this is Janna's idea, not mine? That I have no inten-
tion of deserting everyone and going back to school
at my age?"

"Your *age?* Oh, darling, what has your *age* to do
with anything? If I've taught you nothing else, please

tell me you've learned that age is no excuse for not *living*."

Ryan sat very still, fiddling with his fork, looking down at the table but not really seeing much of anything. Finally he said, "What did the others say?"

"Do you care?" Allie countered, looking slightly sly.

His chest rose and fell as he gave one quick, silent chuckle. "Nope. I don't think I do. Son of a gun—I don't think I do." He stood, kissed the top of Allie's head. "With your permission—and probably without it—I'm going next door to talk to Joe. Make him an offer he can't refuse."

Allie grabbed Ryan's arm, stopping him for a moment. "He's partners with Larry, remember, but as Larry and Linda will be announcing their engagement anytime now if I'm any judge—and I am, remember—I doubt Joe's business partner will mind. Not that you've asked, but Larry and Linda have been in Jamaica together for the last two weeks. As Linda is Matt's sister, Larry will probably see it all as one big happy family. And you people say I don't know how to matchmake, laughed at me when I brought the two of them together for dinner that night Maddy and Joe got back together."

"We're fools, all of us, and should be ashamed of ourselves," Ryan said, kissing her cheek. "And you should run the world. Definitely."

"I do, darling, I *do*," she called after her grandson, who was already halfway out of the room. "Ha! Lucille! Where are you hiding yourself, woman? Get the car keys. I feel like some serious grandmother and housekeeper of the groom shopping!"

* * *

Not surprisingly, Allie was right yet again, as Ryan soon found out.

Minutes later, sitting across the breakfast table next door—with his sister Maddy turning her head from her husband to her brother like a spectator at a tennis match—Ryan learned that the idea of making the Chandler business part of Joe's ever expanding software company had already occurred to Joe. It had occurred to him the moment Allie had suggested it, to be truthful, but since it was a good idea, he'd decided to pretend it had been his own.

"Larry agrees," Joe told Ryan as Maddy removed the silver cover hiding a pile of homemade blueberry pancakes and offered them to both men. "I think he's twice as happy because Linda is Matt's sister and Matt is married to Jess. I mean, soon we'll all be singing 'I'm My Own Grandpa,' but it's fun, isn't it? And, for our sins, Allie's played matchmaker for all of us."

"There's a thought," Maddy said, forking two pancakes onto her own plate and reaching for the syrup. "She's going to be terribly smug, isn't she?"

"I'm having a little trouble with all of this," Ryan admitted, although he was happy to see his confusion hadn't robbed him of his appetite. Maddy made fantastic blueberry pancakes. "None of you cares that I don't want to run the business anymore?"

"Nope," Maddy said, grinning at him. "Why would we? I'll bet all the little girls bring you apples, teach. And Jess says she bets you'll end up as basketball coach, too. Is she right?"

Ryan looked at his sister. Blinked. Smiled. A slow smile that went all the way up to include his eyes. "I've got to go see Janna."

"About time," Maddy said in mock disgust as Ryan all but ran out of the house. "You men. You're darling, but you're so *backward* sometimes. Jess and I have known this would all work out from the very beginning."

"Yes, dear," Joe agreed, then went around the table, picked up Maddy straight out of the chair, and carried her toward the stairs. "Backward we might be, but we're also pretty quick on the uptake, every now and again."

Janna was packing. She didn't want to leave, but it was time to go. Jack had even located and installed the perfect stove, darn him anyway for being so efficient.

She nearly dropped the "priceless" figurine as the door to the apartment opened, hitting against the wall, and Ryan burst into the room.

"Why do you care whether or not I follow my dream, as you call it?" he demanded, walking straight up to her, taking hold of both her arms. "The whole truth now, Janna. All of it. I need to hear you say it, and you need to say it. Why, Janna?"

"Because I never had the courage to follow mine," Janna answered quietly, avoiding his eyes as her heart began to pound in her chest. They'd been good together these past few days. Laughing. Holding each other. Avoiding subjects that caused them to argue with each other. Why did he have to go and spoil everything now, when she had halfway convinced herself that she could leave, take her memories, and not regret what could have been with all of her heart?

"Nope. That's not it. Oh, it sounded good, at the time, and I'm betting there's some truth in there

somewhere. But that's not it. I know you now, Janna.
You'll get around to your art again, sooner or later.
You won't be able to fight it. Those sunflowers should
have told me that, if I'd had half a brain—which I
haven't. Not since meeting you. So, if that's not it,
what is? It's because you care about what I do. You
really *care*. Why do you care so much?''

She bit her bottom lip. ''Because, if you were going to spend the rest of your life denying what you
want most, it would be a bad influence on Zachary.''

Ryan tipped his head to one side, considering this.
''All right, that makes sense. Except that Zach doesn't
know I have the faintest thoughts about teaching, now
does he?''

''He would...if I told him,'' Janna said weakly.
Really, the man was beginning to get on her nerves.
Worse, she was beginning to get on her own nerves.
She'd always prided herself on being truthful. So why
was she having so much trouble being truthful now?

Because you could lose him someday, a small voice
whispered inside her. *Because you know what it's like
to lose someone you love. It hurts. It hurts so bad. It
was just easier to make up reasons not to open yourself to that pain ever again.*

Ryan was looking at her. Waiting. Patiently waiting.

From somewhere even deeper inside her Janna believed she heard Mark whisper to her: *Tell him. Tell
him, darling. It's all right. We had our time. Too
short, yes, but we had our time, our love. Now it's
time to get on with your life.*

Janna blinked, and two perfect tears ran down her
cheeks. Cleansing tears, freeing tears. She had her
memories, and she'd never, never ever forget.

But it was time to make more memories.

"I love you, Ryan," she said at last, then quickly pushed him away. "I want you to follow your dream because I love you, and I want you to be as happy as you can possibly be for as long as that's possible. All right, are you happy now?"

"Getting there," Ryan said, stepping toward her, his slowly curving smile making her long to bop him over the head with something soft and fluffy. "Go on. Why do you love me? I mean, I'm such a stubborn guy, and a coward, remember? Why do you love me?"

Janna pulled herself up to her full height, hitched her thumbs in the back waistband of her faded blue jeans. She stuck out her bottom lip and blew upward, a single curl that had fallen down over her forehead moving in the breeze.

And she told the truth.

"You stood silent and solemn through three verses while Zachary buried the clock, and never cracked a smile or looked bored," she said. "That's for starters."

"Go on," Ryan said, taking another small step in her direction.

"You don't know a caulk gun from first base," Janna added, beginning to feel better. Lighter. Even freer. "You're tall enough to make me feel small and dainty. You kiss better than Brad Pitt, even if I've never kissed Brad Pitt."

He took another step, so that he was standing right in front of her. His smile was beginning to look... hungry.

She liked that.

"Wait, I'm not done yet," she warned, putting up

her hands, somehow finding them pressed against his chest. "If I see you, I get to see Allie and Maddy and Jess and everyone else, and I think I can put up with seeing you so I can be with them. You have a great basketball hoop. The knots on the tire swing are too tight to take out, move the swing back home. Mrs. Ballantine makes me laugh. If you tie a pork chop around your neck, Zach will play with you. And, lastly, I'm pretty crazy about the way I can make you blush, like you're blushing now, big, strong man that you are."

"I'm crazy about Zach," Ryan said, lifting a hand to cup her cheek. His voice was low and rumbling, and did strange things to her insides; strange, lovely things. "And I'm crazy about that amazing hair of yours, and your combat boots, and the way you look in a pair of jeans. I like your smile, and your laugh, and the way you shake me up, give me a new way of looking at the world, at myself. And if you don't agree to marry me, Janna Monroe, I'm probably going to have to camp outside your kitchen until you have no choice but to take me in or paint me to match your lawn furniture."

"That would be purple, with yellow stripes," Janna said, her voice barely a whisper. "I don't think you'd look good in purple and yellow."

"Is that a yes, then?" Ryan was kissing her neck now, and Janna was letting him. Helping him.

"Oh, yes…that's a yes…."

Epilogue

The Fairview Cemetery in nearby Whitehall was home to one of the oldest, if not the very first, Civil War monuments in the country. Located on a grassy hillside, with the monument near the very top of the hill, it towered over the area, its tall sides carved with the names of Union soldiers, four real Civil War cannon surrounding it.

Janna had discovered the monument years earlier, thanks to her friend, George, and she'd shared that discovery with Ryan, who had been amazed to learn of the monument's existence.

None of this, however, explained to Allie why she should be getting out of a white limousine at ten o'clock on a chilly November Saturday morning, a coat over her lovely dress, to watch her only grandson get married.

But then, if she had to have it explained to her, it might take some of the romance out of the thing, so Allie had never asked.

And not that she would have gotten any answers. Janna and Ryan had been maddeningly secretive about the wedding ceremony, only allowing Allie to take over the plans for the enormous reception to be held much later that same day.

The marriage ceremony itself was restricted to close family only.

"Over here, Allie," Joe O'Malley said, taking her elbow and guiding her to a double row of folding chairs that had been set up on the flattest area. "Sit here, next to Jess, who has promised not to move from here without holding on to Matt's arm or else she can't have any cake at the reception."

"He means well, even if he can't believe I still know how to balance on my own two feet," Jessica said, patting the chair next to hers, encouraging Allie and the trailing Mrs. Ballantine to sit down. "Oh, and have you met Sam and Mary? I know Janna didn't think they'd be able to come, but they've managed it. Sam, Mary? My grandmother, Almira Chandler."

Allie twisted in her seat, years of training keeping her eyes from widening, her mouth from dropping open. Sam and Mary Monroe were two of the most *ordinary* people she'd ever seen. Professors, that was what they looked like. Sam Monroe even had suede patches on the elbows of his slightly frayed tweed jacket, and Mary Monroe wore her steel-gray hair in an unbecoming bun.

"How pleased I am to meet you!" Allie cooed, shaking hands with both of them. "I never would have—I mean, Janna's told us *so* much about you both." Wait until she got hold of that girl! How could she have let her be surprised like this! There was a lot more of Allie in Janna than she sometimes liked, not that she didn't adore the child.

"We were in Crete, you know. Beastly cold here, compared to Crete," Sam said, pushing his rimless glasses back up his nose. "Met your boy. Good man. With a real sense of history. Good, good. Well, I must go. Walk the child down the aisle, you know. Then it's off to New York. Fine exhibit of early Croatian artifacts there this month."

Allie gave a vague wave as the man walked off, heading toward a small frame building that had the word Pavilion painted on it. "I think I'm feeling rather light-headed," she whispered to Jessica, who just laughed.

"Just wait, Allie, it gets better," Jessica warned as Joe helped direct the minister to the small area decorated with huge baskets of the palest yellow roses, then took up his seat next to his sister-in-law.

The door to the pavilion opened and Matt and Ryan walked out, headed toward the makeshift altar.

They were both dressed in authentic Civil War uniforms, Matt's the gray of the Confederacy, Ryan's the deep blue of the Union.

"My stars," Mrs. Ballantine whispered. "Don't they look handsome?"

"They do, don't they?" Allie asked, sitting up higher in her chair, groping in her purse for a hankie she'd brought but, until this moment, didn't believe she'd actually use. She wiped at her suddenly moist eyes. "Like something out of an old picture book."

Next out of the door was Zachary, grinning ear to ear as he banged on the drum on his hip, held there by the broad white straps that crisscrossed over the shirt of his blue uniform, his red hair tumbling out from under his blue cap.

"Oh, dear, that does it for me," Mrs. Ballantine said, grabbing the handkerchief from Allie and dabbing at her own eyes.

"Wait," Jessica said in a loud whisper. "It only gets better."

And Jessica was right again. Next to come out of the pavilion was Maddy, looking absolutely splendid in a pale-yellow antebellum gown, its low neck emphasizing the fine swell of her breasts, the pale yellow so very striking against her blacker than black hair. Her tiny yet full figure was made for such long-ago elegance, and Allie had a quick flash of Vivien Leigh's Scarlett in *Gone with the Wind,* and knew that Maddy would have outshone the woman, stealing Rhett right out from under her nose.

"Janna wanted me, too, and Joe," Jessica said, "but Joe said he'd keep me company because, no matter that Janna and Ryan may have meant well, I just couldn't see myself in a hoop skirt right now."

"Good choice," Allie said, then said no more because Zachary was doing a pretty good imitation of a drumroll.

Janna appeared in the doorway, also clad in an antebellum costume, one of softest ivory silk and what appeared to be genuine antique ivory lace. Sam Monroe, looking only slightly bewildered and almost splendid in a long gray wool overcoat with at least three caped collars, the style obviously dating from the Civil War, walked beside her.

Janna's mass of burnished curls was piled high atop her head, with several ringlets falling to one bare pale shoulder.

She carried white roses to the yellow ones Maddy carried, and a circlet of white roses was woven into her hair.

She was beautiful, more than beautiful. She was radiant. Tall, slim, graceful. She walked behind the shorter Maddy, her eyes easily looking over her sister-in-law's head, straight at Ryan.

Allie put a hand to her mouth to stifle a sob. Such love. There was such love in Janna's eyes, such love in Ryan's as he looked back at her.

Everything had worked out so well. After the fact. After the fact, Janna had told Ryan she was already planning to close her small business and get back to her painting. After the fact, Ryan had told Janna he would be selling the company and going back to school to get the classes he needed in order to teach.

After the fact, that fact being that they loved each other, really loved each other, trusted each other, wanted only to be with each other.

But then, Allie reminded herself as she wiped surreptitiously at her moist eyes, she'd always known that, hadn't she?

It was only later, at the reception, when Allie learned that Janna's something new had been her gown, which wasn't all that out of the ordinary.

But the "borrowed" for the ceremony had been ribbons from both Jessica's and Maddy's wedding bouquets, tied onto her own bouquet. The something blue had been the blue-backed cameo locket necklace Ryan had given her as a wedding present.

And the something old had been her combat boots, which she'd worn under the elegant antebellum skirt.

Oh, yes, it was definitely going to be fun having

Janna around. Definitely! Especially as Janna's wedding present to her new husband had been a bright-purple backpack to take to school with him, on which she'd hand-painted a great big smily sunflower face.

*   *   *   *   *

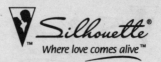

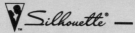

where love comes alive—online...

eHARLEQUIN.com

shop eHarlequin

♥ Find all the new Silhouette releases at everyday great discounts.

♥ Try before you buy! Read an excerpt from the latest Silhouette novels.

♥ Write an online review and share your thoughts with others.

reading room

♥ Read our Internet exclusive daily and weekly online serials, or vote in our interactive novel.

♥ Talk to other readers about your favorite novels in our Reading Groups.

♥ Take our Choose-a-Book quiz to find the series that matches you!

authors' alcove

♥ Find out interesting tidbits and details about your favorite authors' lives, interests and writing habits.

♥ Ever dreamed of being an author? Enter our Writing Round Robin. The Winning Chapter will be published online! Or review our writing guidelines for submitting your novel.

USA Today Bestselling Author

SHARON SALA

has won readers' hearts with thrilling tales
of romantic suspense. Now Silhouette Books
is proud to present five passionate stories from
this beloved author.

Available in August 2000:
ALWAYS A LADY
A beauty queen whose dreams have been dashed in a
tragic twist of fate seeks shelter for her wounded spirit
in the arms of a rough-edged cowboy....

Available in September 2000:
GENTLE PERSUASION
A brooding detective risks everything to protect the
woman he once let walk away from him....

Available in October 2000:
SARA'S ANGEL
A woman on the run searches desperately for a reclusive
Native American secret agent—the only man who can save
her from the danger that stalks her!

Available in November 2000:
HONOR'S PROMISE
A struggling waitress discovers she is really a rich heiress—
and must enter a powerful new world of wealth and
privilege on the arm of a handsome stranger....

Available in December 2000:
KING'S RANSOM
A lone woman returns home to the ranch where she was
raised, and discovers danger—as well as the man she once
loved with all her heart....